HOME *on the* RANCH

HOME *on the* RANCH

A KISS ON CRIMSON RANCH

— ⚔ —

MICHELLE MAJOR

⬙ HARLEQUIN® HOME ON THE RANCH

Recycling programs
for this product may
not exist in your area.

ISBN-13: 978-1-335-45342-6

A Kiss on Crimson Ranch

Printed in U.S.A.

www.Harlequin.com

Michelle Major grew up in Ohio but dreamed of living in the mountains. Soon after graduating with a degree in journalism, she pointed her car west and settled in Colorado. Her life and house are filled with one great husband, two beautiful kids, a few furry pets and several well-behaved reptiles. She's grateful to have found her passion writing stories with happy endings. Michelle loves to hear from her readers at michellemajor.com.

For Jackson. I love you for your heart,
your smile and everything you are.
I'm so proud to be your mom.

Chapter One

Sara Wells gripped the steering wheel of her ancient Toyota and tilted her chin. "Punch me," she said, and squeezed her eyes shut. "Right in the face. Go on, before I lose my nerve."

She heard movement next to her and braced herself, flinching when a soft hand stroked her cheek. "I'd never hit you, Sara, even if I wanted to. Which I don't."

Sara opened her eyes to gaze into the kind, guileless face of her best friend in the world, April Sommers. Her only friend. The friend whose entire life savings Sara had recently lost.

She swatted April's arm. "You should. I

deserve it." A bead of sweat slid between her shoulder blades and she rolled down the window a crack. Her lungs stung as she inhaled the crisp alpine air. "How does anyone breathe around here?" she muttered. "I miss the L.A. smog."

"Go see the attorney. Stop avoiding reality."

"Reality Bites." She paused, then lifted a finger. "1994. Starring Ethan Hawke, Winona Ryder and a very green Ben Stiller. Who would have thought that of the three, Ben Stiller would end up the biggest star? Come on. *Little Fockers?* Are you kidding me?"

"You're doing it again."

Ignoring the soft admonishment, Sara leaned forward to gaze out the car's front window at the row of brightly colored Victorian stores lining Main Street. "Look at that. Warner Bros. couldn't have created a better Western set."

"This *is* the West."

Right.

Crimson, Colorado. Population 3,500 if the sign coming over the pass into town was accurate. Altitude 8,900 feet. Sara blamed the lack of air for her inability to catch her breath.

April rummaged in the sack at her feet.

"Aren't you curious?" She offered Sara an apple. Sara held up a half-eaten Snickers in response.

"I gave up curious a long time ago." She stuffed the candy bar into her mouth. "Along with cigarettes, savage tans, men and chocolate." She swallowed. "Okay, scratch chocolate."

That resolution had fallen by the interstate about four hours into the thirteen-hour drive from Los Angeles. While Crimson was only thirty minutes down the road from the ritzy ski town of Aspen, it held as much appeal to Sara as a blistered big toe.

Sure, it was beautiful if you were one of those back-to-nature types who appreciated towering pines, glittering blue skies and breathtaking views. Sara was a city girl. A blanket of smog comforted her; horns blaring on the I-5 made her smile. In her world, ski boots were a fashion statement, not a cold-weather necessity.

She was out of her element.

Big-time.

"Go on." April leaned over and opened the driver's-side door. "The sooner you talk to the attorney, the quicker we'll be back on the road to la-la land."

Sara's need to put Rocky Mountain May-berry in her rearview mirror propelled her out of the car. She couldn't do that until she met with Jason Crenshaw, attorney-at-law, whose cryptic phone call two days earlier had started this unplanned road trip.

If nothing else, she hoped the money Crenshaw had for her would buy gas on the way back. And groceries. Sara could live on ramen noodles and snack cakes for weeks, but April was on a strict organic, vegan diet. Sara didn't understand eating food that looked like cat puke and tasted like sawdust, but she had no right to question April's choices. If it weren't for Sara, April would have plenty of money to spend on whatever she wanted. And rab-bit food cost plenty of money.

She pulled her well-worn jeans jacket tight and squinted through a mini dust tornado as a gust of wind whipped along the town's main drag. Mid-May in Southern California and the temperature hovered at a balmy seventy degrees, but Crimson still had a bit of winter's chill to the air. The mountain peaks surround-ing the town were covered in snow.

Sara didn't do snow.

She opened the pale turquoise door to the office of Crenshaw and Associates and stepped in, lifting her knock-off Prada sunglasses to the top of her head.

The desk in the reception area sat vacant, large piles of paper stacked precariously high. "Hello?" she called in the general direction of the office door at the back of the lobby.

A chair creaked and through the door came a younger man who looked like he could have been Andy Griffith's rumpled but very handsome son. He peered at her over a pair of crooked reading glasses, wiping his hands on the paper napkin stuffed into his collared shirt.

Sara caught the whiff of barbecue and her stomach grumbled. No food envy, she reminded herself. Noodles were enough for her.

"Sorry, miss," the man said as he looked her over. "No soliciting. Try a couple doors down at the diner. Carol might have something left over from the lunch rush."

Sara felt her eyes widen a fraction. The guy thought she was a bum. Fantastic. She pulled at her spiky bangs. "I'm looking for Jester Crunchless," she said with a well-timed lip curl.

"I'm Jason Crenshaw." The man bristled. "And who might you be?"

"Sara Wells."

Immediately his posture relaxed. "Ms. Wells, of course." He pulled out the napkin as he studied her, revealing a tie decorated with rows of small snowboards. "You know, we watched *Just the Two of Us* religiously around here. You're different than I expected."

"I get that a lot."

"Right." He chuckled self-consciously. "You're a heck of a lady to track down."

"I'm here now."

"Of course," he repeated. "Why don't you step into my office?"

"Why don't you hand over the check?"

His brows drew together. "Excuse me?"

"On the phone you said *inheritance*." She reached into her purse. "I have ID right here. Let's get this over with."

"Were you close to your grandmother, Ms. Wells?"

"No." She could barely remember her grandmother. Sara's mother had burned a trail out of Crimson as soon as she could and had kept Sara far away from her estranged family.

"The heart attack was a shock. We're told she didn't suffer." He paused. "It's a loss for the whole town. Miss Trudy was the backbone of Crimson."

A sliver of something, a long-buried emotion, slipped across Sara's heart and she clamped it down quickly. Shaking her head, she made her voice flip. "It's tragic that she was your backbone and whatnot. I barely knew the woman. Can we talk about the money?"

Another pause. "There is no money." Crenshaw's tone took on a harsh edge. Harsh was Sara's home turf.

Sara matched his emotion. "Then why in the hell did I just drive all the way from California?"

He cleared his throat. "We discussed an inheritance on the phone, Ms. Wells. Not money, specifically." He turned to a rickety file cabinet and peered into the top drawer. "I have it right here."

Great. She and April had driven almost a thousand miles for an old piece of costume jewelry or something. She mentally calculated if she could get to Denver on the fumes left in her gas tank.

He turned back to her and held out a set of keys. "There's some paperwork, for sure. We should talk to Josh about how he fits into the mix. He and Trudy had big plans for the place. But you look like you could use a rest.

Go check it out. We can meet again tomorrow morning."

Tomorrow morning she'd be halfway to the Pacific Ocean. "What place?"

"Crimson Ranch," he told her. "Miss Trudy's property." He jingled the keys.

Sara's stomach lurched. "She left me a *property?*"

Before Crenshaw could answer, cool air tickled Sara's ponytail. She turned as her mother, Rosemarie Wells, glided in with bottle-blond hair piled high on top of her regal head. A man followed in her wake, indiscriminately middle-aged, slicked-back salt-and-pepper hair, slight paunch and cowboy boots that looked custom-made. Sara assumed he was the latest in her mother's long string of rich, powerful, jerk boyfriends.

Could this day get any worse?

Rose slanted Jason Crenshaw a dismissive glance then snapped her fingers at Sara. "We need to talk, Serena."

Sara's stomach lurched, but she focused on the attorney, snatching the keys out of his still-outstretched palm.

"May I help you?" he asked, his eyes a little dazed. Her mother had had that effect on men since Sara could remember. It had been at least two years since she'd seen her mother last, but Rose looked exactly the same as far as Sara could tell. Maybe with a few less wrinkles thanks to the wonders of modern plastic surgery.

"You can ignore her." Sara bit at a cuticle.

"Serena, stop that obnoxious behavior."

She nibbled harder. "This is kind of a coinkydink, Mom. You showing up now." Sara locked eyes with her mother. Rose knew about the will, she realized in an instant.

Her mother's gaze raked her. "You look like hell, Serena."

"Stop calling me that. My name is Sara." She narrowed her eyes but crossed her arms over her chest, suddenly conscious that she was wearing an ancient and not very support-ive sports bra. "Sara Wells. The name you put on my birth certificate."

Her mother's large violet eyes rolled to the ceiling. "The name I had legally *changed* when you were eight."

"I changed it back and you know it." Sara took a step forward. "A monumental pain in the back end, by the way." She cocked her head to one side. "Although it's handy when collections comes calling."

Her mother's nose wrinkled. "I can help you with that, Serena."

"Sara."

Rose ignored her. "Richard wants to buy your grandmother's property." She tilted her head at the aging cowboy, who tipped his hat rim at Sara, Clint Eastwood style.

"I don't understand why Gran left it to me."

"To make things difficult for me, of course," Rose said with an exaggerated sigh. She dabbed at the corner of her eye. "Mothers are supposed to look out for their children, not keep them from their rightful inheritance."

Sara never could cry on cue. She envied her mother that.

"No matter. I know you've gotten yourself into another mess, Serena. A financial nightmare, really. We can fix that right now. Mr. Crenshaw, would you be so good as to draw up the paperwork?" She leveled a steely gaze at Sara. "I'm bailing you out again. Remember that."

Rose had never helped Sara out of anything—contract negotiations, come-ons from slimy casting directors, defamatory tabloid headlines, a career slowly swirling down the drain. The only times in Sara's life her mother had stepped in to *help* were when it benefited Rose at Sara's expense.

"I'm not selling."

"What?"

"Not yet. And not to you, Mother."

"Don't be ridiculous." Rose darted a worried glance toward the cowboy, whose hands fisted in front of his oversize belt buckle. "What choice do you have?"

"I'm not sure." Sara turned to the attorney. "Can you give me directions to the ranch?"

"I'll write them down," he said, and with obvious relief, disappeared into the back office.

"What kind of game are you playing?" Her mother pointed a French-tipped finger at Sara. "We both know you're desperate for money. You don't belong on that ranch." Rose's tone was laced with condescension. "She had no business leaving it to you."

Decades of anger boiled to the surface in Sara. "She did, and maybe if you'd look in the mirror beyond the fake boobs and Botox you'd see why. Maybe she wanted to keep it out of your hot little hands." She leaned closer. "Want to talk about that?"

Her mother recoiled for an instant, then straightened. "You don't have a choice."

"No." Sara's spine stiffened. "I didn't have a choice when I was eight and begged you not to take me on another round of auditions. I didn't have a choice when I was thirteen and I wanted to quit the show after the assistant director came on to me. I didn't have a choice at seventeen when you checked me into rehab for *exhaustion* because the publicity would help the fans see me as an adult."

"If you'd taken my advice, you wouldn't be in the position you are now. I had your best interest at heart. Always."

Sara laughed. Actually laughed out loud in her mother's face. The statement was that absurd. "You tell yourself whatever you need to make it through the day. We both know the truth. Here's the kicker. Right now I do have a choice." She gripped the keys hard in her fist. "Stay away from me, Mother. Stay off of my property or I'll have you hauled off to the local pokey."

"You wouldn't—"

Sara met her angry gaze. "Try me."

She flicked a gaze at Jason Crenshaw, who'd returned to the office's lobby. "I'll be in touch," she said and took the piece of paper he handed her. Without another glance at Rose, she reached for the door, but a large hand on her arm stopped her.

"You're making a big mistake here, missy," the aging Marlboro man told her, his voice a harsh rasp.

She shrugged out of his grasp. She'd been intimidated by far scarier men than this old coot. "What's new?" she asked, and pushed out into the too-clean mountain air.

Josh Travers took a deep breath, letting the fresh air clear his muddled head. He'd been doing trail maintenance on the hiking path behind the main house for over three hours, moving logs to reinforce the bridge across a stream that ran between the two properties. His knee had begun throbbing about forty-five minutes into the job. Now it felt like someone had lit a match to his leg. Josh could tolerate the physical pain. What almost killed him was the way the ache radiated into his brain, making him remember why he was stuck here working himself to the point of exhaustion on a cool spring morning.

What he'd lost and left behind. Voices whispering he'd never get it back. The pain was a constant reminder of his monumental fall—both literal and figurative.

He turned toward the house and, for the first time, noticed a silver sedan parked out front. He didn't recognize the car as any of the locals. He squinted and could just make out California plates.

Damn.

He thought of his daughter, Claire, alone in her bedroom, furiously texting friends from New York.

Double damn.

If his leg could have managed it, he'd have run. Instead, he walked as fast as his knee would allow, trying to hide his limp—just in case someone was watching. It was all he could do not to groan with every step.

By the time he burst through the back door, he was panting and could feel sweat beading on his forehead. He stopped to catch his breath and heard the unfamiliar sound of laughter in the house. Claire's laughter.

He closed his eyes for a moment and let it wash over him, imagining that she was laughing at one of the lame jokes he regularly told to elicit a reaction. One he never got.

He stopped short in the doorway between the back hall and the kitchen. Claire's dark head bent forward into the refrigerator.

"How about cheese?" she asked. "Or yogurt?"

"Really, we're fine" a voice answered, and Josh's gaze switched like radar to the two women sitting on stools at the large island at the edge of the kitchen. One looked in her late thirties, two thick braids grazing her shoulders. She wore no makeup and might have a decent figure, but who could tell with the enormous tie-dye dress enveloping most of her body. She smiled at Claire and something about her made Josh relax a fraction.

His attention shifted to the other woman, and he sucked in another breath. She tapped painted black fingernails on the counter as her eyes darted around the room. Her long blond hair was pulled back in a high ponytail; streaks of—was that really fire-engine red?—framed her face. The same blazing color coated her mouth, making her lips look as plump as an overripe strawberry. He had a sudden urge to smear her perfect pout with his own mouth, as if the most important thing in the world was for him to know if it tasted as delicious as it looked.

His body tightened, and he realized with a start that his knee had company in the throbbing department.

No way.

Her lips parted, and he forced his gaze to her eyes. She stared back at him with an expression that said she knew just what he was thinking.

No how.

Her eyes were pale blue, a color made almost silver by the heavy liner that rimmed them. Her skin was unnaturally pale, and he wondered for a moment if she was into that vampire-zombie junk Claire had told him about. He wouldn't put anything past one of those Hollywood types.

"Josh, look who's here. Can you believe it?" Claire gushed. He studied his daughter, who'd spoken in primarily monotone grunts since she'd arrived at the ranch a month earlier, but now thrummed with excitement.

"Call me Dad. Not Josh," he told her.

"Whatever." She gave him one of her patented eye rolls. "It's Serena Wellens." Claire shot a glance at the women. "I mean Sara Wells. But you know who she is, right? A real-life star here in our kitchen."

"A real-life star?" Josh didn't subscribe to *Entertainment Weekly,* but he was pretty sure Sara Wells hadn't been considered a "real star" for close to a decade now. Josh eyed

Sara, who wore a faded Led Zeppelin T-shirt and capri sweatpants that hugged her hips like…nope. That was not where he needed his thoughts to go.

Sara pushed back from the counter. "Your kitchen?" she asked, raising a brow. "That's not what Mr. Crapshoot told me."

"You saw Jason Crenshaw."

"Yep." She jangled a set of keys in front of her. "Looks like you've got a little 'splaining to do, Daddy-O."

Maybe he shouldn't have questioned the "star" bit. What did he know about Hollywood and celebrities? If a former child actor who hadn't had a decent job in years wanted to consider herself a star, it was no business of his. He knew guys who hadn't gotten onto the back of a bull for decades, but their identity was still wrapped up in being a bull rider.

Not Josh, though.

He'd had his years in the ring. Made a pretty good living at it. Broken some records. Truth be told, it had been his whole life. The only thing he'd ever been a success at was bull riding. But the moment they'd wheeled him out of that last event in Amarillo, his kneecap smashed into a zillion bits, he'd known he was done. His world would never be the same. He walked away and never looked back. Hung up his Stetson and traded the Wranglers for a pair of Carhartts.

People had told him he had options. He could try announcing. Get hired on with a breeding operation. Coach young riders. That last one was the biggest laugh. Just the smell of the arena made Josh's fingers itch to wrap around a piece of leather. He could no sooner have a career on the periphery of riding than a drunk could tend bar night after night. Being that close to the action and not able to participate would kill him.

A couple of times in the hospital and during rehab, he'd almost wished the accident had done the job. His gaze flicked to Claire, who looked between Sara and him with a mix of confusion and worry on her delicate features. She looked like her mother. Both a blessing and a curse, if you asked him.

At the end of the day, she was the reason he'd made it this far after the accident. He wasn't going to let some two-bit tabloid diva mess with his plans.

He forced a smile and turned his attention back to Sara. "About that," he began.

He watched her sense the change in him and stiffen. *Charm, buddy. The groupies thought you had it. Let's see what you've still got.*

He stepped forward and held out a hand. "I'm Josh Travers."

She eyed his outstretched palm like he'd offered her a snake. "Why are you living in my house?"

"Her house?" Claire asked.

Josh turned to his daughter. "Maybe you could head up to your room for a bit?"

"You must be joking." Claire crossed her arms over her chest. "And miss this?"

He made his tone all business. "Now, Claire."

His daughter made a face. "Bite me, Josh. I'm not leaving."

He heard Sara muffle a laugh as he stared down the beautiful, belligerent thirteen-year-old who had every right to hate him as much as she did. He'd been a lousy dad. Almost as bad as his own father, which was quite an accomplishment. He didn't know how to deal with her anger or attitude. Did he play bad cop or go soft? He barely knew his daughter, and in the weeks she'd been living at the ranch, he hadn't made much progress on repairing their relationship. One of the laundry list of things he should feel guilty about.

"Fine." He turned to Sara, who smiled at him. At his expense. "Trudy and I were partners."

"Is that so?" She wiggled her eyebrows. "Very *The Graduate,* although you don't strike me as much of a Dustin Hoffman. And from what I remember, Gran was no Anne Bancroft."

Josh shook his head and glanced at the hippie lady. "What is she talking about?"

She gave him a sympathetic smile. "Sara likes movie analogies. Ignore it."

He wished he could ignore this entire situation.

"Dad, is this our house or what?" Claire asked.

He sighed. "Technically, it belonged to Trudy."

Sara jingled the keys again.

"And now to you," he admitted.

"Oh. My. God." Claire let out a muffled cry. "I have no home. Again." She whirled on Josh. "You told me we were going to stay here. I could paint my room. Are you going to send me off like Mom did? Who else is left to take me?"

"No, honey. We *are* going to stay here. I'll work it out. I'm not sending you anywhere."

She sniffled and Josh turned to Sara. "Your

grandmother and I were opening a guest ranch. She owns the house, but I have the twenty-five acres surrounding it. We back up onto the National Forest so it's the perfect location for running tours. I've been here since the fall working on renovations and booking clients. Guests start arriving in a couple of weeks."

Sara looked from Claire to Josh, her gaze almost accusatory. "Does it make money?"

He tried to look confident. "It will. I've sunk everything I have into the place." *Everything I had left after medical bills,* he added silently. "Trudy was going to help for the first season. I planned to buy her out with my half of the profits."

"But now the house is mine."

Josh nodded. "I don't expect you to hang around. I'll cover the mortgage. At the end of the summer, I can take the whole place off your hands."

"Why can't you buy it from me now?" Her gaze traveled around the large room.

"The bank wants to see that it's a viable business before they'll approve my loan. Trust me, it's a good plan. Trudy and I worked it out."

She looked him up and down. "Trudy isn't here anymore."

"I know," he agreed, feeling the familiar

ache in his chest as he thought of the woman who'd been more of a mother to him than his own. He wondered how difficult Sara was going to make this for him. He'd known Trudy's granddaughter had inherited the house. Josh had gone directly from the funeral service to the bank to see if he had any options. He didn't. He needed time and a bang-up summer to make this work. Otherwise, he might as well burn his savings in a bonfire out back. There was no Plan B.

"What if I want to sell now?"

His gut tightened. "Rose got to you already."

"How do you know my mother?"

"She and her land-developer boyfriend have been here a couple of times. The guy wants to tear down the house and build luxury condos on the property. Make Crimson a suburb of Aspen. What an idiot."

Claire took a step forward. "Are you going to let us stay or should I start packing?" She eyed both Sara and Josh as she bit her lip. "Because all my stuff is folded and in drawers where I want it."

He heard the desperation in her voice, knew that despite her smart mouth, his daughter was hanging on by a short thread these days.

As much as he didn't want to admit it, they had that much in common. He'd promised to take care of her, make up for his past mistakes. The ones he made with her and those he'd buried deeper than that. He needed this summer to do it.

"Claire, I told you—"

"I know what it's like to want a place to call home," Sara said quietly, her attention focused completely on Claire. Her eyes had gentled in a way that made his heartbeat race. For a moment, he wished she'd look at him with that soft gaze.

Claire blew out a pent-up breath and gave Sara a shy smile, not the sarcastic sneer she typically bestowed on him. His heart melted at both her innocence and how much she reminded him of another girl he'd once tried to protect.

Sara returned the smile and his pulse leaped to a full gallop. *Don't go there,* he reminded himself. Not with that one.

"Can you give your dad and me time to talk?" Sara asked. "To work things out? Maybe you could show April around." She pulled her friend forward. "She's into nature and stuff."

"Come on," April said. "Can we walk to the pond I saw on the way in?"

Claire nodded. "It's quicker to go out the back."

As she passed, Josh moved to give his daughter a hug. She shrugged away from his grasp. One step at a time. He'd seen her smile, even if it wasn't at him.

"Thanks," he said when the back door clicked. "I'm sure we can—"

"Cut the bull."

So much for the soft gaze.

She folded her arms across her chest. Josh forced himself to keep his eyes on her face.

"I don't want to hurt your kid, but I don't have time to play *Swiss Family Robinson* for the summer. I need money and I need it now. If you want to make a deal, what do you have to offer?"

His adrenaline from a moment ago turned to anger and frustration. "I put everything I had into buying the land and fixing up the place. I've paid for marketing, a website, direct mail. We've got a real chance of making this work." He raked his hands through his hair. "It has to work."

"I'm not about to…" She stopped and cocked her head.

"What? Not about to what?"

"Do you hear that?"

A sudden sound of pounding filled the air.

"That sounds like—"

He turned as Buster, his oversize bloodhound, charged down the hall, galloping toward the kitchen.

"Buster, sit." The dog slid across the hardwood floor and ran smack into Josh's legs, all enormous paws and wiggly bottom.

"Buster's harmless."

He looked back at Sara, now crouched on the butcher-block counter with wide eyes. "Keep that thing away from me."

He felt a momentary pang of sympathy for her obvious fear, then glanced at Buster and smiled. "Looks like I've got you right where I want you, Hollywood Barbie."

Chapter Two

So much for being cool, calm and in control.

"This isn't funny." Sara hated that her voice trembled.

Josh bent to rub the giant beast's belly. The dog was deep brown with a wide ring of black fur around the middle of its back. Its eyes were dark, at least what she could see under the wrinkles that covered its head. It yawned, displaying a mouth full of teeth and flopped onto the wood floor. One pancake-size ear flipped over his snout. Outstretched, it was nearly as long as she was.

"This is *Buster*," Josh said with a laugh. "He wouldn't hurt a fly."

"That dog looks like he could eat me for breakfast."

"Lucky for you, it's nearly lunch."

"You are *so* not helping here."

"I like you better up there. You're not chewing me out."

"I wasn't chewing—" She stopped and met his gaze, now lit with humor. "You're living in my house."

"I explained that."

"I need to sell it."

"Sell it to me." He stepped closer. "At the end of the summer."

Fear had taken most of the fight out of her. "What am I supposed to do in the meantime?"

He held out a hand. "You could start by climbing off the counter."

She watched Buster, who'd begun to snore. "I don't like dogs."

Josh's low chuckle rumbled through her. "I never would have guessed."

She didn't move from the counter. "The fourth season of the show, I got a dog." She closed her eyes at the memory. "My character, Jenna, got a dog. It hated me on sight. The first day on set it bit me. Twice. I wanted to get rid of it, but the director's girlfriend was the dog trainer. She said it could sense my fear. That it was my fault the dog growled every time I came anywhere near it. Of course, the thing loved Amanda. Everyone loved Amanda."

"Who's Amanda?"

"Amanda Morrison."

"The movie star?"

"Highest-paid woman in Hollywood three years running. Back in the day, she was my sidekick on the show."

She expected a crack about how far the mighty had fallen. He asked, "How long was the dog around?"

"Lucky for me, the director was as big of a jerk with girlfriends as he was with me. By the end of the season, the dog was gone."

"Did it ever warm up to you?"

She shook her head. "I got faster at moving away after a scene. I never realized how much my fingers resemble bite-size sausages." She blew out a breath. "Animals and me, we don't mesh."

She looked away from the sleeping dog, surprised to find Josh standing next to her beside the kitchen island.

This close, she could see that his dark brown eyes were flecked with gold. A thin web of lines fanned out from the corner of them. He was tall, well over six feet, with broad shoulders that tapered into a muscled chest under his thin white T-shirt. Unlike most guys in Southern California, Josh didn't look like he'd gotten his shape with an expensive gym membership or fancy trainers. He'd clearly worked for it. Real sweat kind of work. He wasn't bulky, but solid. Although he wore faded cargo pants and gym shoes, he still gave off a definite cowboy Mr. Darcy air.

If Mr. Darcy had an unnervingly sexy shadow of stubble across his jaw, a small scar above his right eyebrow and a bit of a crook in his nose like he'd met the wrong end of a fist one too many times. A dangerous, bad boy Mr. Darcy.

It was one thing to slip on giving up chocolate; bad boys were quite another. She'd had enough of bad boys in her time. They swarmed L.A. like out-of-work actors.

His gaze caught hers, and it took her a moment to remember what she was doing in this house in the mountains, cowering on the kitchen counter.

He reached out a hand and she took it, still a little dazed. "It's not going to come after me?" she asked, throwing a sharp glance at the dog.

"I'll protect you," he answered, his tone so sincere it made her throat tighten. Among other parts of her body.

Off balance, she scrambled down, the heel of one shoe catching on the corner of a drawer and sending her against the hard wall of his chest. She stepped back as if he'd pinched her, but he didn't release her hand.

His calloused fingers ran the length of hers. "Nothing like sausages," he said with a wink.

She snatched her hand away and moved to the other side of the island, thinking the altitude was making her light-headed. Praying it was the altitude.

"Where's Claire's mother?" she asked. As she'd hoped, the spark went out of his eyes in an instant.

"She was having some problems—personal stuff—needed a little time to get herself back on track. So Claire's here with me."

"For how long?"

He shrugged. "As long as it takes. Why do you care?"

"I have experience with bad parents. It can mess with you if you're not careful."

"Are you careful, Sara?"

"I'm broke," she said by way of an answer.

"Like I said before, I need the money from the sale of this house."

He hitched one hip onto the island. "You own the house, but it's only on a quarter-acre lot. I've got all the land surrounding it. Your part isn't going to be worth much without the land."

Crenshaw hadn't mentioned that. "Then why is my mother's latest boyfriend so hot for it?"

Josh took a moment to answer. "Basically, I'm hosed without the house. I can't run a guest ranch without a place to put the clients. If he gets you to sell to him now, I won't have an income stream this summer. And without money…"

"I know what happens without money."

"Right. Here's the deal. Assuming things go well when the season starts, I can pay you double the mortgage for the next three months. That should get you through until I can secure the loan."

"Why should I do it your way?"

He lifted one brow. "Because you're a kind and generous soul," he suggested.

She answered with a snort. "Is that the best you've got?"

"It will make your mother crazy mad."

"That's a little better."

"Listen, Sara. Your gran was one of the best. She was nice to me when I was a kid and a good friend since I got back. While I don't know the terms of her will, it doesn't surprise me that she left you the house. She loved this place and she talked about you a lot."

"I barely knew her."

He nodded. "One of her biggest regrets was that she didn't do more for you. Help you out when things got rough."

"Woulda, shoulda, coulda," Sara said, but turned away when her voice cracked. "You know, I spent a summer here right before the show got picked up."

"Trudy told me."

"It's funny. I don't remember a thing about that time."

"Look around the house...maybe it will come back to you. I'm going to find Claire. Whatever you decide, Sara, your grandmother did love you. You should know that."

She waited until his footsteps faded, then let her gaze wander after quickly checking that the dog remained sleeping on the floor.

The house was more an oversize log cabin, exposed beams running the length of the walls and across the ceiling. Their honey color gave the interior a cozy warmth in the late-afternoon sunlight. Across from the kitchen was a family room with high ceilings and a picture window that framed a million-dollar view of the craggy peaks surrounding the valley.

An overstuffed sectional and several leather armchairs sat in front of a wall of bookshelves with a large flat-screen TV in the center. Nothing looked the least bit familiar to her, and she wondered whether Josh had gotten the new gadgets or if her grandmother had been into cutting-edge electronics.

Did all of it belong to her, or would he strip the house if she sold? Maybe she should have spent a little more time with the attorney. Sara had been so angry when her mother had shown up that she clearly hadn't gotten the whole story about this place.

Couldn't anything be easy? she wondered as she made her way up to the second floor. She peeked her head into the first bedroom. Posters of pop stars and young actors lined the walls. A blue-and-purple comforter with peace signs covered the bed. Claire's room.

Next to that was a bathroom, and then came the master bedroom. She stayed at the threshold, not wanting to venture into the room where Josh slept. Even from the doorway, she could smell the same scent he'd had today—a little woodsy, a little minty and totally male. She didn't want to be affected by his scent, by anything about a man who was entirely too rugged and rough for her taste.

She stepped quickly to the end of the hall. The final bedroom had soft yellow walls with lace-trimmed curtains, a four-poster bed and an antique dresser next to a dark wood ladder-back chair. She took a breath as she walked to the front of the dresser, skimming her fingers across the lace doily that covered the top. Framed photos lined one side, mostly her grandmother with people she didn't recognize, friends probably.

A few showed her mother as a girl, and in one she was a young woman carrying a baby: Sara. Sara was just a toddler in the photo and she smiled at the camera, one hand raised in a wave. Sara didn't remember a time before the endless rounds of auditions, cereal commercials and eventually prime-time celebrity. She'd been ten when *Just the Two of Us* first aired. The next seven years had been spent in a constant cycle of filming, promotions and off-season television movies.

It surprised her that her grandmother had

none of her promo photos displayed. The only photos Rose had framed in their two-bedroom condo were publicity shots. Sara's hand trailed over a photo album that sat in front of the frames. She traced the jeweled beads that had been glued to the cover in the shape of her name. A sliver of memory trailed through her insides.

She sat down on the bed and flipped open the album. Her heart skipped a beat as she gazed at the first page. It was a picture of her holding a giant ice-cream bar, mouth covered in chocolate, grinning wildly at the camera. In the next picture, she was on a trail, her blond hair pulled back in two pigtails and wearing an oversize cowboy hat. Her jaw dropped as she continued to turn the pages. Pictures of her feeding horses, a shot of her curled in a tight embrace with her grandmother. She read the caption below the photo: "Sara's first annual summer visit" written in Trudy's loping penmanship.

As she'd remembered, her mother had gotten a small part in a blockbuster Steven Spielberg movie that year. A part that had ended up on the cutting room floor. Shortly after that movie, Rose had switched her considerable energy to Sara's career. Which explained why first annual had quickly become one and only. Although Sara had no memory of this place, clearly she'd spent some happy times here.

And that was what her grandmother knew of her: Sara as a normal girl, before Rose had created Serena Wellens, deeming Sara too basic a name for the superstar she was destined to become. Even at the height of her fame, Sara had never identified herself as Serena. She'd been content with plain old Sara, although her mother had reminded her on a regular basis that fresh-faced Saras were a dime a dozen in Hollywood.

She'd had to become someone else, someone more special than who she was.

Being Sara wasn't enough.

She sniffed as a tear fell onto the photo, then wiped at it with her thumb. Taking a deep breath, she stood. One thing she had in common with her more glamorous persona was that neither one of them did tears.

She placed the album back on the dresser and started down the hall, but her gaze caught on a poster on the far side of Claire's bedroom wall. It was a picture of Albert Einstein with a famous quote underneath.

Sara wasn't one for inspirational quotes.

Actions spoke louder than words in her world. She didn't know any details of Josh and Claire's relationship, but it had been very clear that it wasn't good. As she looked around the bedroom, she wondered what would happen if they didn't get this summer together.

She shouldn't care. Neither of them were her business. A month ago when she'd landed back on the tabloid covers and lost her most recent waitressing job, she'd vowed to mind her own business. Take care of herself. She was number one.

But she'd seen something in Claire's eyes that she hadn't remembered feeling for way too long. Hope. Even as the girl had looked at Josh with anger and resentment, there'd been a spark of something that said *don't give up on me*. Josh didn't seem like a quitter, so maybe they'd have a chance. The chance Sara had never had for a normal life.

How could she take that away?

Her heart raced as she made a decision. She hurried down the stairs and out the back door before she came to her senses.

Josh, Claire and April were walking across the field behind the house. She waited until they got close. "Good news," she announced. "I'm staying."

Josh stopped dead in his tracks. "What do you mean *staying?*"

"Here. For the summer. I'll make sure you have a good season, and then sell it to you in September."

Claire did a little dance around him, making his head spin more than it already was. "That's so great," she gushed. "Now maybe this summer won't be as awful as I thought."

"Hey," he said, pulling her around to look at him. "You think it's going to be bad?"

She shrugged then wiggled out of his grasp. "Not as much as before."

He squeezed his eyes shut for a moment and counted to ten. When he looked at Sara again, she'd walked toward April and taken the other woman's hands in hers. "I know I messed up and I'm going to make it right for you. The cowboy here offered to pay me double the mortgage for the next three months. That should at least cover your expenses for the summer. If Ryan ever calls..."

He didn't bother to try to follow their conversation. "I said I'd pay you double to *leave.* Go back to California. Let me run things here. You'll get your money."

She shot him a dubious look. "Hell, no,

partner. I'm sticking right here, and I'm going to make sure things go right."

"I've got it under control," he ground out.

"Oh, yeah? That kitchen looks pretty decked out. I'd guess my gran was going to do the cooking."

He nodded, not liking where this conversation was going.

"Best blueberry muffins ever," Claire added.

"And now?"

"I'm interviewing people," he admitted. "Do you cook?"

She rolled her eyes. "That's not my point."

"Which is?"

"You need help."

"Not from you, I don't."

"I could handle the kitchen," April offered quietly.

His gaze shot to April, who was looking at Sara.

"You don't have to do that," Sara told her. "You have a life."

April smiled. "I could use a little break, and I'm sure I can sublet the beach house for the summer."

"Is this because of losing the studio? You could teach some other place. Rent another space. You know your clients would follow you anywhere."

"That's the beautiful thing about yoga. I can take it anywhere, too." She gave Josh a hopeful smile. "I could even offer a few classes on the ranch. To start the morning, maybe."

Sara glared at him over April's shoulder, nodding vigorously. "That would be perfect," she said. "Your veggie burgers are the best. Josh, is there a Whole Foods anywhere around here?"

"A whole what?"

"They just opened one on the way to Aspen," Claire piped in. "But Dad only shops at the Red Creek Market."

April nodded. "It's important to support local businesses. I'll drive into town tomorrow morning and see what we can work out."

"When are the first guests arriving?" Sara asked no one in particular. "We'll need time to plan out the right menus. Do you have lists of food preferences and allergies? That sort of thing?"

"Hold on," Josh bellowed, raking his hands through his hair. "Hold on! No one is making veggie anything at my ranch. People book trips looking for action and adventure, not airy-fairy spa treatments and yoga classes. They want to fish and race ATVs, hike four-teeners and mountain bike the local trails. I'm the boss around here. I do the hiring. I make the plans. I'm the one—"

He looked at the three women, April's gaze a little hurt, Claire's eyes narrowed and Sara shaking her head just a bit as she chewed on her full lower lip.

"I'm the boss," he repeated quietly, willing it to be true.

"Don't be a hater," Claire mumbled.

"A what?" He rubbed his temples. "Never mind."

"You don't have a chef, do you?" Sara asked, her voice too knowing for his taste.

"I'm interviewing cooks."

"And who's planning all the so-called adventures?"

"I am."

"And leading the fun?"

Was it his imagination or did her gaze stray to his knee? "That's me, too. Got a problem?"

She took a step closer to him. Across the bridge of her nose, under who knew how many pounds of makeup, he could see the faint outline of freckles. Distracting freckles.

Freckles he wanted to trace, wondering if her skin was as soft as it looked.

"Face it, cowboy," she said, bringing him back to the moment, "you need us."

"I don't need anyone."

He heard Claire snort.

"Jerk," Sara said under her breath.

A dull pounding started behind his left eye, matching the throbbing of his leg. "Fine. But this isn't the Ritz. If you're here, you work."

She tossed her streaked hair. "I've been working since I was eight years old."

He suppressed a growl. "Not the kind of work that involves a catered lunch."

"You think you know me so well."

"I know your type."

"We'll see about that." She gave his shoulder a hard flick. "I'll give it until Labor Day, Lone Ranger. If you can't get the bank loan approved by then, I'm taking the next best offer."

He studied her luminous blue eyes, their depths cold as an alpine stream. "Deal."

They glared at each other, and though he kept his eyes on her face, he noticed that her chest rose and fell unevenly and a soft pink flush rose to her cheeks. His own breath quickened, and without knowing why, he leaned in and enjoyed watching her big eyes widen.

The hippie chick clapped a few times, breaking the weighted silence. "If that's settled, we should think about planning. I'll start with dinner."

He forced his gaze from Sara's. "The local diner has decent takeout."

April laughed. "I'll cook tonight. Think of it as an official interview."

He nodded. "There are six smaller cabins on the property. Four of them are two bedrooms. You can have your pick."

"Can't they stay in the house with us?"

"No," Josh and Sara said in unison.

"Whatever," Claire mumbled.

Sara turned to his daughter. "Would you show me the other cabins?" She glanced warily at the thick pine forest that surrounded his land. "I want the one least likely to be invaded by critters."

Josh expected Claire to offer up one of the flip comebacks she gave him every time he asked for her help. To his surprise, she gave Sara a genuine smile. "Sure. Will you tell me about all the stars you know in Hollywood?"

A momentary cloud passed through Sara's

eyes before she smiled brightly. "Oh, sweetie, I've got some stories for you."

Claire giggled. Actually giggled as she led Sara toward the row of cabins that sat in front of the small stream at the back of the property.

"Unbelievable," he said under his breath.

He heard April laugh again and whirled on her. "What?" he demanded. "What is so funny?"

She took a step back, palms up. "Nothing at all. Do you want to discuss menus while I check out the kitchen?"

Josh recognized a peace offering and was smart enough to take it. "Let's go," he said, and headed for the house.

Chapter Three

Sara glanced up from the computer in Crimson's small-town library. It had been three days since she and April had arrived in Colorado. Word spread fast that former starlet Serena Wellens was in town for the summer. A steady stream of locals had stopped by the ranch for neighborly visits. Of course the disappointment in meeting a once-upon-a-time celebrity in real life had been obvious from the comments she'd received.

"You looked taller on TV."

"You were so pretty when you were younger."

"Do you still talk to Amanda? Can you get her autograph?"

Her favorite had been from the town's mayor, who'd blurted, "I read you overdosed a year ago. I think I sent your gran flowers as a condolence."

It was a good thing the ego had been pummeled out of her years ago. Otherwise, the blatant disapproval might have done her in.

She watched a couple of teenage boys stare at her from behind the bookshelves at the far end of the room. She pulled off her headphones and winked in their direction. Her smile broadened as they ran away, books clattering to the floor in their wake.

"You enjoyed that a little too much."

She started at Josh's deep voice and swiveled her head to see him approach. Quickly, she clicked the mouse to minimize the screen and turned to block his view completely. "The picture-book section is on the other side," she said with a huff.

To her dismay, he gave her a knowing grin. "Whatcha doin', Hollywood?" His lazy drawl made her insides twist in a way she didn't like.

She shrugged in response. "Checking out the gossip sites. A little Facebook. April's meeting with the owner at the market to arrange food deliveries to the ranch so I'm killing time."

He craned his neck to peer over her shoulder. "I think you looked me up on Google."

"You wish," she sputtered as a voice sounded through the headphones that she'd dropped to the desk.

"Josh Travers does it again. It's a new record and another amazing showing from bull riding's reigning king." Applause and cheers echoed in the background.

Heat rose to her cheeks as Josh arched a brow.

"Fine. I was curious. So what. Don't tell me you haven't looked me up, too."

"I wasn't sure which site I liked better— serenawellensforever.com or sarawellsstinks. com."

"*Just the Two of Us* fans didn't love it when I changed my name. They thought they knew me when I was Serena. Like my name mattered."

"It mattered to you."

"Reigning king, huh?" she asked.

"That was a while back," he said with a smile, as if he knew she was changing the subject.

She studied him for a few moments. "I saw pictures of your accident."

His back stiffened. "Pictures exaggerate."

"The bull landed on top of you."

"They got him off quick."

"Does your knee still bother you?"

"Not really."

"Liar," she whispered. "Do you miss it?"

"Not really."

"Did you ever see that Jim Carrey movie *Liar, Liar* when he can only tell the truth?"

He scratched his jaw. "I don't think so."

"It's an interesting idea, don't you think? Even if he tried to tell a lie, it wouldn't come out of his mouth."

He just watched her.

"I'm kind of babbling."

"Yep."

He did that to her, she thought. He was such a presence. Big and broad and totally in his space—in her space. People in L.A. were always planning what came next, even if it was a trip to the mall. But Josh stayed in the moment no matter what he was doing. He kept busy, and to her eternal gratitude, she hadn't seen much of him other than watching him walk across the property early in the morning to take care of the horses, then catching glimpses of him throughout the day.

Yesterday, he'd spent most of his time on the roof of the largest cabin, replacing worn shingles. When the sun moved high overhead and the temperature rose with it, he'd taken off his shirt. Much to her dismay, Sara found herself staring out the window in the office far too often. It had been a while since she'd had a man in her life, but she figured she could get her wayward hormones under better control than that.

Here in the quiet intimacy of the library, those little buggers took flight again. With Josh standing in front of her, his faded T-shirt stretched over his chest and sculpted arms, she could imagine...

Nope.

She *did not* imagine. She'd given up her imagination when she'd abandoned her dreams, around the time she began filling in *waitress* under the occupation heading on paperwork.

This man was all that stood in the way of the possibility of reclaiming her life, or at the very least, creating a new one. The money from the sale would allow April and her to start over. The only view she'd let herself imagine was Josh Travers disappearing in her rearview mirror.

"So what *are* you doing here? Did they run out of *Playboy*s at the general store? I don't think the library has a subscription."

He shrugged then held out a book. The cover read *Talk To Your Teenager Without Losing Your Mind.*

"That's a mouthful."

"The librarian recommended it."

"It's nice that you're willing to read a parenting book."

"Claire hates me."

"She doesn't hate you," Sara argued as she stood and gathered her things.

"This morning after you and April left I asked her to help me feed the horses. You would have thought I was waterboarding her." He scrubbed a hand over his face. "I thought all girls loved horses."

"Not *all*," she clarified.

"Thanks, I've got that now. One of the mares sniffed her and she freaked out. I laughed a little."

"You laughed at her?"

He smacked the heel of his hand to his forehead. "So shoot me. I didn't mean it. She threw a bucket of grain at me, screamed that she hated the ranch, she hated her mother and most of all she hated me. My dad would have whipped my butt if I'd thrown a fit like that."

"What did you do?"

"Nothing. She ran back to the house. I finished in the barn and came here."

Sara led the way out of the library and into the warm afternoon air. She glanced up at the bright blue sky, still surprised at how much this small mountain town resembled a movie set. "She doesn't hate you," she repeated.

"Did you hear anything I just said?" Josh asked, his face incredulous.

"She's a teenager. Hormones running rampant and in a new place with a parent she barely knows. Give her time."

He looked like he wanted to argue then took a breath. "Time. Right. When are you coming back?"

Sara checked her watch. "I'm supposed to meet April in a half hour."

"What's the deal with the two of you? She was willing to follow you to Crimson and seems happy to do her part at the ranch. That's quite the package deal."

"I don't know much about the rodeo circuit, but in Hollywood finding someone who truly cares is a rarity." Sara took a breath before continuing. "I met April about the time my career was starting to tank and my personal life was just as messed up. She stuck with me through the bad stuff, and I did the same with her when she had her own troubles. She doesn't belong in L.A. anymore. If a summer at the ranch can help her see that, all of this would be worth it. She deserves happiness more than anyone I know."

He studied her for several moments. She struggled not to fidget under his scrutiny. "You're a good friend," he said finally.

"Oh, I'm the bee's knees, and don't you forget it." She laughed, trying to ignore the intensity of his gaze. "I need to stop by that clothing store at the end of the block. My L.A. wardrobe doesn't really work here."

Josh took a long look at the outfit she wore today. A shapeless black-and-white-striped sweater dress over skintight black jeans that zipped from knee to ankle. Her shoes, Converse trainers, were at least more practical than the heeled boots she'd worn yesterday. Without the heels, she was pixie-size, and if it wasn't for the heavy makeup lining her eyes and dark wine-colored lipstick, she might have passed for a teenager herself.

A lock of neon hair slipped from her newsboy cap, and she tucked it behind her ear. Josh's gaze locked on the soft blond wisps at the base of her neck, and he was momentarily fascinated to imagine her natural honey color.

That was the kind of woman he was drawn to: natural, sweet and compliant. A woman who'd bake pies from scratch with strawberries fresh from the garden. The kind of woman he could grow old with, reveling in a normal, boring, run-of-the-mill Ozzie and Harriett life. Not a bitter, bossy, snappish former diva.

No attraction to that type.

Not at all.

He fell in step beside her.

"You mean Feathers and Threads?" Other than T-shirt shops and the fishing shop, which sold outdoor gear, that was the only women's clothing store in town.

"I prefer to think of it as Cowgirl Duds R Us."

He chuckled. "It's not bad. Do you think you could help me pick out something for Claire? Maybe a necklace or earrings?"

She slanted him a curious look.

"A peace offering. For this morning."

"Buying your way out of the doghouse?"

"Whatever it takes." They reached the

end of the block. "I need to stop in at the fly shop first. I ordered vests and waders for the ranch."

She didn't slow her pace. "See you in a few."

He watched her walk away and couldn't help but notice that the way her hips swayed under the striped dress was all woman.

Damn.

The bells over the door of Feathers and Threads chimed as he walked in fifteen minutes later. He glanced around but didn't see Sara. Maybe she was in the dressing room.

"Hey, Rita," he called to the shop's owner, who stood behind the counter with a young salesgirl and a cluster of customers.

He'd brought Claire here when she'd first arrived in town. His daughter had taken one look at the racks and announced she'd be buying her clothes from the Hollister website. The morning after, he'd taken Rita to coffee as an apology for Claire's rudeness.

Too bad she'd read more into that than he'd meant. She'd all but suggested a quickie in the back room of the store. When he'd refused, she'd still found excuses to stop by the ranch several times, dropping off sparkly tops and hand-knit sweaters for Claire. To his relief, Claire had kept her snide comments to herself, and he'd been able to avoid Rita as much as possible. That was another reason he wanted to come in here at the same time as Sara—someone to distract Rita.

"Hi, Josh," she cooed. "Can I help you with something?"

"I'm picking up a gift for Claire. I'll look around."

"Let me know if you have questions," she answered and turned back to her conversation.

He silently congratulated himself and headed toward the jewelry case at the back of the store. Rita and her gaggle of customers laughed softly as he walked by. Snippets of conversation drifted his way.

"…rode hard and put away wet."

"No wonder she can't get work. Who'd want to see that on the big screen?"

"Is it just me or has she had her lips done?"

"Doesn't belong in Crimson, that's for sure."

Josh concentrated on the necklaces as unease skated around his chest. He glanced in the small mirror above the jewelry case and spotted Sara standing behind a sale rack.

As Josh turned toward the group of women,

the conversation behind the counter continued, louder now. The women made no attempt to be discreet.

"I read she was into drugs for a while," one of the customers offered, bending forward so that Josh got too much of a view of her ample backside.

Eyes widened within the group. "Did you see track marks?"

"I can't get past those raccoon eyes," another woman said with a snicker.

"It looks like she hasn't seen the sun in years," Rita answered. "Maybe we should send her down to Nell's salon for a makeover."

Maybe you should shut your mouth, Josh thought. He glanced at Sara in the mirror, expecting to see steam rising from her ears. He was surprised she hadn't come out swinging already. Instead, he watched her swipe under her eyes and return a blouse to the rack, her hand shaking a bit.

"I wouldn't wish that hot mess on anyone," the younger salesgirl said, sending the other women into peals of laughter.

Josh felt his blood pressure rise along with the volume of giggles. He looked back to Sara, and her gaze met his in the mirror. For a single moment her eyes were unguarded and he saw pain, raw and real, in their depths. She blinked and shuttered them, turning the glare he'd come to know so well on him in full force. She shook her head slightly and backed away from the clothes rack.

Now, he thought. *Cut them down now.* She turned to a display of knit tops and picked one out at random. He watched her carry it to the front of the store. The women looked her up and down, not hiding their judgment and contempt.

"Just this," she said quietly, keeping her eyes forward. "You have some lovely things in the store."

"They all have security tags," Rita answered as she punched a few keys on the cash register.

"Of course."

Josh's temper hit the roof. How could Sara let that group of catty witches fillet her without defending herself? Where was the sarcastic, no-holds-barred woman he'd already come to expect? Hell, he hated to admit it, but he actually looked forward to their verbal sparring to break up the monotony of his day.

But this? This was total and complete bull.

He grabbed two necklaces from the rack and stalked to the counter.

"What do you think of these?" he asked as he slammed them onto the glass top.

Rita jumped back an inch then pasted on a broad smile. "With Claire's gorgeous skin the turquoise will—"

"I'm not talking to you," he interrupted, unconcerned with how rude he sounded. "Which one, Sara?"

"The butterfly charm," she answered immediately. "The turquoise on the other one is dime-store quality."

"I beg your pardon?" Rita sputtered.

Sara didn't make eye contact with either of them, only dug in her purse for a wallet.

That a girl, Josh thought. *Just a little more.*

"Claire trusts your opinion," he continued conversationally. "I think she was sold the moment Gwyneth called to see what she should wear to her movie opening."

"Gwyneth Paltrow?" the salesgirl asked, her tone taking on a fraction of respect.

Sara's fingers tightened around her purse and she sliced a dead-meat look at him.

He forced a chuckle. "It's like Hollywood is one big sorority." He pointed to Sara. "Her phone is ringing every ten minutes. Julia needs to know where to find some kind of boots. Sandra's texting about a brand of fancy-pants jeans."

Rita raised an eyebrow at Sara. "And they're calling *you?*"

When Sara didn't answer, Josh spoke quickly, "Like you wouldn't believe."

Sara pulled out cash and handed it to Rita. "For the sweater." She didn't acknowledge Josh's comments or Rita's question.

Rita took the money, studying Sara. "I'm ordering for fall in a couple of weeks. Maybe you could stop by and take a look at the lines. We're not as exclusive as Aspen, but I still want to offer current trends. I'd appreciate a fresh opinion."

"Fresh?" Sara questioned. "As in fresh off heroin?" She yanked her sleeves above her elbows and held out her arms for inspection. "No track marks, ladies. Needles were never my thing."

Two of the women giggled nervously and backed away from the counter. After an awkward pause Rita said, "If you've got time, stop back later in the month."

Sara blew out a breath. "Give me a break," she mumbled, and left the store, leaving the bagged sweater and change Rita had placed on the counter.

Josh quickly paid for his necklace, grabbed Sara's bag and followed her into the warming afternoon. He caught up with her half a block down the street.

"What happened in there?"

She rounded on him. "Why don't you tell me, Mr. Name Dropper?" She jabbed at his chest, her voice rising. "Since when are you an expert on celebrity fashion? Not one damn person has called my cell phone since I got here, famous or otherwise. And you know it."

"Excuse me for trying to help. Those women were out for blood, and you were about to open a vein for them."

"You should mind your own business," she countered.

"Who *are* you right now?" He took a deep breath, needing to clear his head. It didn't work. Not one bit. "All you've done since the minute you walked into my house—"

"My house."

"*The* house," he amended. "All you've done is bust my chops. If I look at you wrong, you read me the riot act, give me one of those snide remarks or smart comebacks you're so damn good at." He pointed in the direction of Rita's store. "You didn't say one word to those ladies in there."

She rolled her eyes. "You took care of it all on your own."

"Somebody had to. It was too painful to watch your slow death."

"Julia, Gwyneth? Even if I was in L.A., do you think one of those women would give me the time of day? They are A-list, Josh. I'm beyond Z. You have no idea what you're talking about."

"Rita didn't know that."

"*I* know it." She scrubbed her hands over her face. "I'm a has-been. A nobody. You don't get it. What those women dished out was nothing compared to what I hear every single day in California. At the grocery. The dry cleaners." She laughed without humor. "At least back in the day when I could afford dry cleaning. I've been a waitress now for the same number of years I was a paid actress. Do you know how many customers gave me career advice, hair tips, dissed my makeup, my boyfriends, all of it? Nothing was off-limits. I can take it, Josh. I don't need you to swoop in and rescue me."

"Excuse me for trying to help."

"I don't *want* help. This isn't *Pretty Woman*

meets mountain town. I'm not Julia Roberts shopping on Rodeo Drive. You're not Richard Gere on the fire escape."

"Why do you do that?"

Her eyes narrowed. "Do what?"

"Throw out movie plots like they compare to what's happening. This is real life, Sara."

"I'm well aware."

He shook his head. "I thought you were a fighter."

"No," she said quietly. "I'm a survivor." With that, she turned and marched down the street away from him.

Chapter Four

Sara didn't say much on the drive from town, content to let April ramble about her meeting with the man who ran the local farm cooperative. She gazed at the tall pines that bordered the winding highway, continuing to be awed by her surroundings. The vivid colors, woodsy smells—the vast magnitude of every inch of this place.

She thought about Josh's "real life" comment. Sara knew real life. Real life was struggling to meet her rent every month, praying each time she used her debit card that her bank account wasn't overdrawn. She had to admit there was something about Crimson that felt—well, authentic. In L.A., life was about who you knew, where you could get a table, which plastic surgeon you frequented. She glanced in the rearview mirror, wondering for a moment about the last time she'd gone anywhere without full makeup. Her war paint, as she'd come to think of it.

Was it possible she could have a brief reprieve from battle in this small mountain community?

As Sara drove down the narrow driveway toward the ranch, she spotted a large black SUV parked in front of the main house.

"If that's my mother…" she muttered under her breath.

April patted her knee. "You can deal with your mother. You're a fighter."

The car almost swerved into the ditch. "Did you talk to Josh?" Sara accused her friend once she was back on the dirt road.

"No," April answered slowly, her dark eyes studying Sara. "What's going on with you two?"

"Nothing."

"I can feel the vibes. They aren't *nothing*."

"You're imagining it."

"He's hot."

"Go for it," Sara suggested. "Maybe he'd relax if he got a little something."

April chuckled. "You know that after my divorce I swore off men, at least until I've found someone who's worth the time and effort. So I don't *go for it* anymore. Besides, maybe *you* could relax if…"

"Not going there."

"We'll see."

"You think you know me so well."

"I've known you since you were fourteen."

The studio had hired April to be Sara's fitness coach when she'd put on a few pounds during puberty. Sara counted that decision as one of the few blessings from her years as a sitcom star. Without April's gentle guidance, Sara might have added "eating disorder" to her long list of personal issues.

Nine years older than Sara, April had quickly become Sara's soul sister and best friend. When April's stuntman husband left her a few years later during April's grueling battle with breast cancer, Sara had been more than willing to see her friend through months of chemotherapy and radiation treatments and the nasty divorce that resulted.

Neither woman had been lucky in the relationship department—another fact that, despite their different outlooks on life, bonded them deeply.

"You only think you know me. I'm a mystery wrapped in a puzzle clothed in an enigma," Sara told her friend with a wry smile.

"Right."

Sara parked the car next to the SUV. "Are you trying to distract me from the probability of another scene with *Mommie Dearest?*"

"Is it working?" April asked, reaching for the door handle.

Sara grabbed her arm. "Have I told you today how sorry I am you're in this predicament with me?"

April shrugged. "Things happen for a reason."

"Don't go all *Sliding Doors* on me. The reason your savings account was wiped out and you lost the yoga studio is because I'm a gullible idiot, a loser and the worst friend in the world. We're stuck in high-altitude Pleasantville for the summer, thanks to me."

"Sara…" April began, her tone gentle.

Sara thumped her head against the steering wheel. "Maybe I was wrong to agree to Josh's plan for the summer. If I sold to Mom's latest sugar daddy we could be back in California next week."

"Back to what?"

"Our lives."

"Neither of our lives was that great to begin with, and you know it. Besides, what about Josh and Claire?"

"Not my problem."

"I guess that's true," April admitted. She pushed open the passenger door. "But we're not going to get anywhere sitting in this car. If you want to hear your mom out, that's your decision. You have to take control of this situation."

"Lucky me," Sara answered, and started toward the house.

Sara walked through the front door, waiting for the scent of White Diamonds, the perfume her mother had worn for decades to hit her. She smelled nothing.

She turned the corner from the foyer and stopped so suddenly that April knocked into the back of her. She stood perfectly still for one moment, then launched herself across the family room at the man who stood on the other side of the couch.

"I'm going to kill you," she yelled, reaching out to wrap her fingers around his neck.

Strong arms pulled her away and she was

enveloped in a different scent—one that even in her anger still had an effect on her insides. "Settle down," Josh whispered in her ear.

"Let me go," she said on a hiss of breath. She fought, and his arms clamped around her, pressing her against the solid wall of his chest. After a minute she stopped struggling. "Let me go," she repeated. "I'm not going to hurt him."

Slowly, Josh loosened his hold on her. For the briefest second, Sara fought the urge to snuggle back into the warmth that radiated off his soft denim shirt, to bury her face into the crook of his neck and simply breathe.

She stepped away, needing to break their invisible connection, and straightened the hem of her long shirt. "You've got a lot of nerve showing up here, Ryan. Unless you've got my money and April's, too, you can crawl back under the rock you came from."

"Hi, Sara." Ryan Thompson, her onetime business partner and long-ago ex-boyfriend flashed a sheepish smile. "I came to apologize." He held out his hands, palms up. "To beg your forgiveness. Go ahead, attack me if you want. I deserve it. Whatever it takes to put this behind us."

Sara felt her temper building but kept her

voice steady. "What it will take is you handing me a check for two hundred thousand dollars. The money it will take to repay April for losing the studio."

Ryan looked past her to April. "Do you, at least, forgive me, April? You understand, right?"

"I understand *you,* Ryan" came April's taut response.

His brows furrowed and he turned his attention to Sara again. "I messed up. I'm sorry. I'm going to make it better."

"By writing a check?"

He sighed. "You know I can't do that."

Sara knew a lot about Ryan Thompson. They'd met when she was nineteen.

Her career had stalled; audiences did not want to see another childhood star grow into a bona fide actor. She'd had a couple of box office flops, lost roles in several Lifetime movies to former cast members of *90210* and could barely get casting directors to meet with her for even supporting roles. She'd briefly thought of applying to college until her mother had informed her that with the quality of on-set tutoring she'd received, she'd been lucky to get her GED.

Her mother, who was still managing her

at the time, had come up with the brilliant idea of sending Sara to rehab for undisclosed reasons.

Although the closest she'd come to an addiction was a great affinity for Reese's cups, Sara had been legitimately exhausted for months and welcomed a break from the Hollywood rat race.

Rose thought the publicity would make people see Sara as an adult, and if they didn't get specific about an addiction, the backlash would be manageable. The whole Drew Barrymore comeback—maybe even a book deal.

It hadn't worked. At all. She'd been blacklisted by every major studio, and her stalled career had gone down the toilet completely. But she'd loved her time at the secluded facility, morning meditation classes and long walks through the desert trails. On one of those solitary walks, she'd met Ryan, a hot young director who'd blown a huge wad of his last project's budget on his gambling addiction. The producers had sent him to the Next Steps treatment facility for a month-long program. As far as Sara could tell, he was the only other patient at the center not half crazed with withdrawal symptoms or buying drugs from the cleaning crew.

They'd been fast friends and had even tried a romance for about a millisecond. Ryan was prettier than Brad Pitt in *Thelma and Louise* and higher maintenance than a full-blown diva. He loved women, could flirt the pants off the Pope's sister and was as good at monogamy as he was at staying away from the blackjack table.

They'd remained close, and while he'd had a couple of critical and box office hits, Ryan continued to be a master of self-sabotage, finding it impossible to resist the lure of Las Vegas's shiny lights.

He'd been clean a year and a half when he'd approached Sara about forming a production company together. She was at the end of her rope with bad waitressing jobs and potential projects falling through. He presented a well-thought-out business plan, complete with spreadsheets, a list of potential investors and a movie script that had *award* written all over it. One with a lead role that made Sara literally salivate with need.

She'd agreed, and for months they'd hit the pavement, calling and setting up meetings to try to make this new dream a reality. After one of the major investors backed out, Sara'd complained to April, who'd offered to take a second mortgage on her yoga studio and give the money to Sara. April had a solid client list of California high rollers and had even been offered her own DVD series working alongside one starlet yoga devotee.

At first Sara had resisted her friend's offer, but April was confident in Sara's ability to make the production company a success. April was the only person who knew that Sara had been taking classes part-time at UCLA and was close to earning a business degree.

She and April planned on franchising the studio, and April's particular brand of yoga and one hit movie could help finance the expansion. Sara saw her chance to create a career away from Hollywood that would both fulfill her and give her the respect she craved.

That was before Ryan fell off the wagon again, blowing all their money on a weekend in Vegas. In less than a month, Sara had lost her savings, her apartment, her latest job and almost her friendship with April.

Now Ryan stood in front of her, offering to *make it better*. She'd trusted him once and wouldn't make that mistake again.

"If you can't write a check, how could you possibly make anything all right again?"

"The financing is almost set. I've got a new

director interested. One who wants you for the lead. He's in Aspen for a few weeks. I just need to get hold of his people and set up a meeting with the two of you." His eyes shifted to April. "I'll get your money back. All of it."

Sara shook her head. "No way. We're done, Ryan. I don't trust you. I don't want to work with you. I don't want you anywhere near me."

"Sara, please," he pleaded, his voice a soft caress just short of a whine.

"She said no, bud." Josh had been so quiet where he stood a few feet behind her, she'd almost forgotten he was there.

Almost.

"I wasn't talking to you, Roy Rogers."

Sara saw Josh's fists bunch at his sides. "Well, I'm talking to you," he said, and took a step forward.

She put up a hand. "It's okay, Josh."

She'd been friends with Ryan long enough to know the pain and regret in his eyes were real. She wouldn't admit it, but it got to her. That was Sara's problem. She was a sucker for lost causes. Having been one for so many years, she could smell desperation on a person like some people could sniff out a good barbecue.

"I'm sorry," Ryan said again.

"You didn't even call. I had to find out from your assistant."

"I went straight from the casino to another stint in rehab." He offered a sheepish smile. "I'm a little more self-aware now, at least."

"Some good it did me."

"Give me a chance, Sara."

She blew out a breath and tried to ignore Josh seething next to her. "Fine. Call me if you get a meeting."

Ryan gave her a bright smile. "That's great. I'll—"

"In the meantime, you can help out around the ranch. Aspen's not that far and I know you have time on your hands. There's lots to do before the guests arrive."

"Hell, no." Josh sliced the air with one hand. "He's a lazy, no-good, designer-jeans-wearing pansy, and he's not touching anything in my house."

Sara whirled on him. "As I remember, this is *my* house."

"You know what I mean."

"I do," she said with a sniff. "And I don't like it." She turned to Ryan. "You'll work,

Ryan. And not as in making reservations. The real thing. Start paying off your debt."

The frown he gave her said he wanted to argue but knew he didn't have a leg to stand on. "Sure. I'll do it. This is a guest ranch, right? What do you need? Someone to charm the clients. A wine sommelier, perhaps?"

She grinned. "A prep cook."

"A what?"

"Someone to help April in the kitchen."

April coughed loudly. "No, no, no. I don't need him, don't want him, won't have him."

Sara studied her friend. April was the kindest person she'd ever met. She didn't have a bad word to say about anyone. She'd give the coat off her back to a complete stranger. She'd expected April to take on Ryan like another one her charity cases. After all, April had been taking care of Sara for close to a decade. April's typically peaches-and-cream complexion had gone almost beet-red, and her chest rose and fell in frustrated huffs as she glared at Ryan.

He'd cost April her business and most of her savings, but even when Sara'd first shared the awful news, April had taken it in stride. She never lost her temper or got ruffled.

Until now.

She waited for Ryan to turn on his almost irresistible charm, offer April one of his trademark lines, smooth talk her into agreeing. Instead, he looked at Josh.

"Could you use a hand with maintenance?"

Josh shook his head.

"Grass to cut?"

"Nope."

"Horse droppings to scoop?"

"Nothing."

Ryan's squeezed shut his eyes. "I can't be completely useless. I'm done with useless."

Sara threw a sharp glance in April's direction. "Come on," she mouthed silently.

April growled low in her throat. "You can help. But you'll do what I say, which mainly involves staying out of my way."

To Sara's surprise, Ryan nodded, then stepped forward and wrapped her in a tight hug. "I *am* sorry."

"Make it better with April," Sara whispered.

"She hates me."

"Do you blame her?"

"I'm a good guy. With a little problem."

"Ryan."

"I need to get back to Aspen today." He leaned back and scrubbed his hand over his face. "But I'll be back and I'll try."

Sara glanced to where April stood, but her friend was gone. "Try hard," she told Ryan. "April deserves to be happy."

He ran a finger across her cheek. "We all do."

"If you say so," she answered. They both knew she didn't mean it.

Josh watched Ryan head toward the front door. His plan had seemed so simple a few months ago. Move back to his small hometown and make a new life on this secluded property. Work at the ranch would give both he and Claire the home and stability he needed. He'd be able to forget his past, the pain of his accident and losing his career—the only thing he'd ever cared about in his life.

With enough hard work, he'd be so exhausted he wouldn't miss the smell of the arena, would stop aching for the feel of a thousand-pound bull beneath him and the adrenaline rush that came with those seconds in the ring.

With enough patience, his daughter would stop looking at him like he was the enemy.

Now he had three California misfits crowding his space. Josh didn't do people and their problems. He had friends, sure. Other bull

riders who were like him, happy to spend
time drinking beer and watching old foot-
age. Once guys left the ring and made homes
and families for themselves, he usually lost
touch. He was a loner and liked it that way.
No complications.

The woman who walked over to the picture
window at the far end of the family room was
the biggest complication he'd ever met. She
complicated his life. What happened to his
insides when he watched her was a problem
he sure didn't need.

He took a few steps toward her, not close
enough to smell the scent that always surrounded her—some strange mix of honey and
cinnamon—sweet with a bit of kick. But close
enough that she couldn't *not* be aware of him.
He wanted her to notice him as much as he
did her.

"Do you two have a thing going?" he asked
casually.

She looked over her shoulder at him. "You
mean Ryan?"

"Who else?"

"Does it matter?"

A muscle ticked at the side of his jaw. "Stop
answering my questions with questions." He
hooked his thumbs into his belt loops. "My

thirteen-year-old daughter is right down the hall from him. I don't want her waking up to any moaning and groaning next door."

One side of her mouth kicked up. "What if Ryan's at my cabin?"

He fought the urge to growl. "I don't need a soap opera played out in front of the clients."

She turned to him fully. "I don't do soap operas." Her eyes narrowed. "What makes you think I'm a moaner?"

Only the fact he'd spent the past three nights imagining the sounds she'd make when she was in his arms, under him, wrapped around him.

He took a step closer, so near that her subtle scent surrounded him and he could feel her breath against his jaw. His fingers reached out and pushed a wayward lock of streaked hair behind her ear. He'd only meant to touch her that little bit, but she turned her cheek, ever so slightly, into his palm. Her warm skin tempted him, called to his inner need. It wasn't a fight he could possibly win.

He brought his other hand up to cradle her face, tracing the edge of her lips with a calloused thumb. Her eyes remained glued to his mouth, and as he came nearer they drifted closed.

The desire to kiss her raced through him like a runaway train, almost knocking him back with its speed and strength. He needed to know if she tasted as sweet as she smelled, if her mouth was as soft as her skin. This prickly, snappish woman who played it so tough on the outside had sparked something in him he'd never felt before. Because he had a feeling that on the inside she was soft and warm. He craved knowing that side of her.

Josh tried to pull away, but he'd never been much for self-preservation instincts. This moment was no different.

She made a noise somewhere between a sigh and a moan.

He was a goner.

"I knew it," he whispered against her mouth.

"Why are you still talking?" she asked, her eyes dark with the same desire he knew was reflected in his.

He pressed his lips to hers. Although he'd known she'd taste amazing, he wasn't prepared for his body's reaction to her. Electricity charged through him as he brushed his tongue across the seam of her lips. He forced himself to keep the kiss gentle when what he wanted was to wrap his arms around her and carry her to his bedroom.

"I don't want to do this," she said on a ragged breath.

He stilled. "Do you want me to stop?"

"Lord help me, no." Her arms twined around his neck, drawing him closer.

What a hypocrite, to complain that his daughter might catch wind of her and Ryan when Josh was ready to get naked in front of an oversize window.

The window. Claire. The thought of Claire seeing him play tonsil hockey with Sara made him pull away from her.

"What's the matter?"

He rested his forehead on hers and drew in several steadying breaths. "Everything. This summer is about Claire. About starting over with her. A second chance."

"Second chances," she said, her voice impossibly quiet. "I get that." The next moment she pushed hard on his chest. "You know what you are, Lone Ranger?"

He shook his head as she started past him, wondering how she could go from soft and pliant to prickly in less time than he could stay on the meanest bull. "What's that, Hollywood Barbie?"

"A tease."

Fighting words. She'd probably chosen

them purposely to break the spell between them, but he couldn't let it go. He grabbed her wrist and swung her around to face him. "You'd better take that back. Now."

She shook free of his grasp. "You won't let anyone in and you'll throw out any excuse in the book so you don't have to." Her eyes glinted, daring him to argue.

His gaze locked on hers, and he let her see how much he craved her. Her breath caught. She took a small step back.

"Do you want in, Sara? Really?"

She looked at a point past his shoulder for a few moments, and when her eyes finally found his, she shook her head. "I want out. Out of Colorado. Out of debt. Out of owing people."

The right answer for both of them, Josh knew, but a sliver of pain sliced across his chest. He wasn't the kind of man women took a chance on. He had nothing to offer except a wild night between the sheets and a wave in the morning.

Even if she didn't know it, he could tell Sara needed a man who would stick.

Joe Hollywood upstairs wasn't it, but neither was Josh.

"It's better this way," she told him. "No complications."

Right.

She tapped her fingers against her jaw as if deep in thought. "I don't like you that much anyway," she said finally. "You're not my type."

"Could you stop waving red flags in front of me?" He dug his hands deep into his pockets to keep from reaching out to her again. Every time she made some kind of ridiculous comment, he itched to prove her wrong. Over and over again.

As if sensing his intentions, she took another step away. "Sorry. No red flags. I have some voice mails to return, so I'll see you later. Or not. Probably not."

"Are we still in good shape?"

Her brow arched.

"Bookings," he clarified. "Guests. Good shape with actually making money this summer." He hadn't wanted to turn the office side of the ranch over to her, but as the start of the season got closer, it became harder to balance the preparations on the property with the work involved in making reservations and talking to potential customers. Sara had insisted that customer service was her strong suit, and despite her sassy attitude with him, so far she'd been a whiz. In less than a week, she'd organized the jumble of paperwork in the office, confirmed their current reservations and followed up with a half-dozen prospective clients.

The best part was that Josh's cell phone, where he'd had the office calls forwarded, had stopped ringing every ten minutes. He'd actually been able to get a lot of projects done. He felt almost ready for guests to arrive.

"We're in better than good shape. I just confirmed a family reunion for six nights at the end of June. There's only one weekend in July still open and August is full." She studied him. "You did an excellent job with the marketing. I guess there was a write-up in *Sunset* magazine recommending the ranch. That's quite a bit of publicity."

He shrugged. "I know an editor there."

She leaned in closer. "Must be an ex-girlfriend because you're blushing."

"I don't blush."

That elicited a full-blown laugh. "If you say so."

The sound of her laughter flowed through him. He grinned back at her. The moment grew quiet again, just the two of them watching each other. The heat in his cheeks took a nosedive south.

She blinked and her lips thinned. "I'm going to the office now."

"Gotcha."

"Don't follow me."

He tipped his head. "Wouldn't dream of it."

She headed for the other side of the house and the two rooms he'd converted to central operations with a little too much speed for a natural gait.

It looked as if she was running away.

Good. Maybe that would save them both.

Chapter Five

The crash from the floor above made Sara jump out of her seat. She rubbed her eyes and bent to retrieve the stack of papers that had spilled off the desk.

After spending the past few days buried in the office or driving back and forth to town for supplies before the first guests arrived, her eyes felt like sandpaper and her back ached. The time sequestered away from everyone was necessary, she told both herself and April, who'd brought trays of food into the office at regular intervals. For the most part, April had kept her opinion to herself, only dropping one or two pointed questions about the real reason Sara was in self-induced isolation.

Sara wasn't ready to admit she was avoiding anyone in particular. Definitely not Josh. Or Ryan, with his continuous stream of apologies and the puppy-dog eyes he kept shooting her.

Another loud thud came from upstairs, this one actually shaking the framed pictures on the office walls. It had to be Ryan, Sara thought with an accompanying curse. He must know she was working, and she guessed this was his ploy for her attention. She'd convinced herself it wasn't going to work until the telltale clatter of glass breaking reverberated through the ceiling.

She muttered another curse and stalked up the stairs. As she made her way down the hall, the sound of muffled crying came from behind one of the closed doors. Claire's room.

Sara knocked softly, then peeked in when no one answered.

"Claire, are you okay?"

Claire sat on the floor at the foot of the bed, her head resting against knees drawn tight to her chest. "Go away," she whispered, her voice clearly pained.

Good idea, Sara thought. That was exactly

what she wanted to do, retreat back to her own office and not get involved in one more person's life. Her gaze caught on the nightstand that had been knocked on its side. That explained the crash. Next to the broken lamp was a framed photo, broken glass surrounding it. Claire smiled from the picture, cradled in the arms of a woman—a drop-dead gorgeous woman—who seemed vaguely familiar.

Sara stepped into the room for a closer look. She recognized Jennifer Holmes, international supermodel. In the past decade, Jennifer had graced the covers of countless fashion magazines and several Victoria's Secret catalogs.

"Is this your mother?" she asked, carefully lifting the frame from the carpet. "She's beautiful." She found a wastebasket beside the dresser and dumped the pieces of glass into it.

"I hate her," Claire mumbled. "She doesn't care about me at all."

"From this picture, she looks like she does."

"Duh." Claire lifted her tearstained face. "She's a supermodel. She can make herself look however she wants for a camera. That isn't real."

Sara knew there could be a big difference between what the camera showed and reality. "What makes you think she doesn't care? Tell me what's real, Claire."

The girl stared at her for several seconds, mouth pressed tight together. Then her eyes filled with tears. "What's real is that she's on some yacht in France with her new rockstar boyfriend. She told me she was getting help. For her drinking and stuff. She's supposed to be putting her life back together so I can live with her again." Claire sucked in a ragged breath, her words spilling forth like the tears that ran down her face. "And she's not. She won't. She doesn't care."

"Maybe she's—"

"I saw it on a gossip website. Pictures of her in a bikini with a guy's hand on her butt. I called her cell phone. She tried to tell me she was at the rehab place." Claire stood and flopped onto the bed. "*After* I saw the website. She's a liar. I asked her if I could come to where she was and she said no. She needs a break." Claire hiccuped and swiped at her cheeks. "A break from *me*."

Sara's heart melted. "Claire, I'm sorry—"

"I hate it here. I don't know anyone. I don't have any friends. Dad act likes we're going to do all this bonding, but he's always working. He barely says two words to me when he's around. It's like he doesn't know what to talk about." She shook her head. "How can I be so bad that neither of my parents want to be around me?"

"Oh, honey." Sara sat down next to the bed and wrapped one arm around the girl's shaking shoulder. Claire stayed stiff and then, with a sigh, sank against Sara.

"It's me," she repeated.

"It's absolutely not you." Sara gave Claire's arm a gentle squeeze. "I know for a fact that your dad loves you very much. He works so hard so he can make the ranch into a home for the two of you."

"It's not going to be much of home when you sell it," Claire said miserably.

Touché, Sara thought with a mental groan. "Whatever happens," she answered without addressing Claire's comment, "he wants to be with you. He's trying to do what's best because of you."

"He doesn't even like to be around me."

Sara squeezed her eyes shut, thinking of the love, longing and confusion in Josh's eyes when he looked at his daughter. "How long did your dad ride bulls?"

"I don't know. Forever," Claire mumbled. "I think since he was like seventeen or something."

"That's only a few years older than you. And how old was he when you were born?"

"Eighteen. My mom was, too."

"Yeah, well. Take it from someone who knows—young parents don't always know what they're doing. Your dad is trying. That has to count for something."

"Was your mom young when you were born?"

"Nineteen." Claire sniffed, and Sara dug in her pocket for a tissue. "Here, use this."

Claire blew hard then said, "She's really pretty. Your mom. She came to the ranch a few weeks ago. Tried to kick Dad and me out."

"That sounds like Mom."

"Are you close with her?"

Sara laughed softly. "Not exactly. You're changing the subject."

"I'm good at that." Claire shifted away from Sara and smiled a little.

"Me, too." Sara reached out a finger and ran it along Claire's cheek. "Have you talked to your dad about how hard it's been here for you?"

Claire shook her head. "I can't."

Sara watched her without answering.

"I don't want to make it a big deal. I guess it's not that bad," Claire said with a sigh. "I mean, I like the mountains. And how the air smells. Like it's…"

"So clean it almost hurts," Sara finished.

"Exactly." Claire picked at an invisible spot on her jeans. "And Brandon's okay."

"The kid who helps your dad in the barn?"

"He's fifteen. His family owns the property across the highway. He's kind of nice."

"And cute."

Claire looked up, pink coloring her cheeks as she met Sara's gaze. "Do you think so?"

"He's got those great big blue eyes, right?"

Claire sighed. "And that smile. He'll actually talk to me. But he's got a girlfriend, I think."

"You can still hang out when he's here. Just friends. I bet your dad would love an extra hand in the barn."

"I don't know anything about horses."

"Just like he doesn't know anything about what teenage girls are into. It's up to you, but I know your dad does care about you. He wants you around. That counts for something. Maybe if you seemed interested in something he knew about, it could help with that bonding you mentioned."

"I wouldn't be in the way?"

Sara smiled. "April and I get in the way. Ryan is always in the way. You're the one Josh wants around."

"I think he wants you around, too," Claire said softly, then asked, "Is Ryan your boyfriend?"

"Absolutely not."

"Do you have a boyfriend?"

"Nope."

"Do you want one?"

Josh's face came to mind, and Sara tried to ignore the shiver that curled through her belly at the thought of his mouth on hers. "I've given up on men."

Claire studied her, looking suddenly older than her thirteen years. "Aren't you a little young for that?"

"I'm twenty-eight. That's like one-foot-in-the-grave time in Hollywood."

Claire nodded as if she understood. "My mom turned thirty-one last year. That's when she started to freak out. Party more. She gets Botox and some other wacky stuff." Claire stood and looked in the mirror above the dresser, pinching two fingers to the bridge of her nose. "She said I could have my nose done as a sweet sixteen gift. That'll be cool. I might look a little more like her and she'll…"

Sara turned Claire to face her. "Listen to me. You are perfect the way you are. Plastic surgery isn't going to change your relationship with your mother."

"You don't know—"

"I do know. I spent years jumping through hoops to win my mother's approval. Guess what? Never happened. Maybe it never will. I hope it does for you, Claire. I hope your mom gets healthy and realizes how precious you are to her. Until then, I know your dad loves you. Even if he isn't great at showing you how much."

"I just want to fit in here," Claire said miserably, her green eyes, so like Josh's, welling again.

"I know, sweetie."

"Would you take me shopping sometime?" Claire asked. "None of my clothes are right for Colorado, you know?"

Sara thought about the women in Feathers and Floss. "Are you looking for Wranglers and studded belt buckles?"

"No." Claire laughed. "Just clothes to hang out in. If you don't have time, I understand."

Sara gave her a quick hug. "I have time. How about before the weekend? I'll drive us down to Denver. We can make it a girls' day out. Go to lunch. Get our nails done."

"Really?"

"Of course, I may only be able to afford one sock, but we'll do our best."

"Dad has money. I could ask if we can use his credit card."

Sara almost choked from laughing so hard. "I bet he'd love that." She pushed the hair off Claire's innocent face. "I pay my own way. But, heck, yeah, we'll get his card for you. A shopping trip is one thing dads are always good for."

"Was your dad good for that kind of stuff?"

Sara's father had been a nameless stuntman on one of her mother's B movies. An on-set fling for Rose, who hadn't even told him she was pregnant and had never shared his identity with Sara.

"I don't know my father."

"Oh. I guess it's good that Josh wants me to live with him anyway."

"He doesn't like it when you call him Josh."

Claire grinned. "I know."

"How much did you see him before this summer?"

"A couple of times a year when he had time off from the tour. He'd come to my school and take me out to dinner. He sent me presents from the road. Lots of stuffed animals and things like that. I'd never been to the rodeo until…" Claire wrapped her arms tight around her chest. "The accident was my fault. Did you know that?"

Sara had read a half-dozen articles about the horrific accident that had ended Josh's career. It still made her sick to her stomach to think about the images she'd seen on You-Tube. But none of the reports had mentioned Claire. "Why do you say that?"

"I was there." Claire scrunched up her face. "Mom was having a bad time. It was winter break and she was stuck with me. She found out there was an event a few days before Christmas and flew us both down there. I think she wanted to dump me with him for the holidays. She didn't tell him we were coming. Right before he came out of the gate, he looked up and saw me. It broke his concentration." Claire drew in a shaky breath. "They let the bull go right at that moment and…" Her voice broke off as she shook her head. "The whole arena was silent when it happened. I thought he was dead. The bull was so big and it landed right on him."

"Claire." Sara drew the girl into another tight hug. Sara had been through some bad stuff as a kid, but this poor girl gave her a run for her money in the bad-childhood department.

"They took him to the hospital straight from the event. I didn't see him again until he showed up on the last day of spring semester." Claire wiped her cheek against Sara's sleeve. "If I hadn't been there, he'd still be riding."

"It wasn't your fault," Sara whispered against the girl's head. "It was a terrible accident. But not your fault. Not your fault."

"But I—"

"Have you and your dad talked about what happened?"

Claire didn't answer.

"I'm sure he doesn't blame you."

"He should."

"You need to talk to him."

"No," Claire whispered. "I don't want to hear him tell me I ruined his life."

Josh sagged onto the wall outside his daughter's bedroom and swallowed against the bile that rose in his throat. He'd come to find her minutes ago but stopped short when he'd heard her conversation with Sara.

He didn't blame Claire for the accident. His break in concentration was his own fault. He'd been riding bulls long enough to know his focus should be zeroed in on the thousand pounds of angry animal between his legs. But when he'd seen Claire, he'd been thrown. Literally and figuratively.

Apparently, they'd both paid a price for his lapse in focus.

In his mind, he'd hoped she hadn't seen much or understood how bad it had been. Hoped her mother would whisk her away before she realized how serious it was. Jennifer had probably been too tipsy to understand the extent of the damage. But not Claire.

He had a hazy memory of trying to smile even as he felt his leg shatter, thinking that if his daughter could see him he didn't want to frighten her. He hadn't wanted her to know how scared he had been. Even now, that thought kept him rooted to his spot in the hall when his heart knew he should be the one with his arms around her, comforting and soothing her.

He'd waited until he could hide his injury before he'd come to see her, thinking that would be easier for both of them. Since he'd brought her to the ranch, sometimes he'd catch her staring at his right knee, especially toward the end of the day when exhaustion and overuse made it more difficult to hide his slight limp.

He wanted to be strong for her, not weak and half-broken. Bending forward, he rubbed at his leg, willing the pain to go away. He straightened and thumped on the wall as he walked to the end of the hall. "Claire," he called, coming back toward her room. "Are you up here?"

He made some more noise before poking his head in her room. She sat on the edge of the bed with Sara next to her. While she smiled at him, her eyes were red and puffy from her tears. "Hey, Dad," she said cheerfully, a sure sign that things were very wrong.

Sara watched him as if his face gave away the fact that he'd been eavesdropping. Impossible, he thought, but kept his gaze on Claire. "It's a gorgeous day," he said to his daughter. "I thought we could take an ATV up to Bitter Creek Pass, check on the trails and maybe have lunch."

Her smile faded. "I don't think so."

He took a breath and made his tone light. "Come on. It'll be fun. Just you and me and a ton of horsepower."

She scrunched up her nose. "Those things are so loud and they go really fast."

"That's supposed to be the fun part," he said, trying not to sound frustrated.

He let his eyes drift to Sara, who looked at

him with a hint of sympathetic smile. "Can I come, too?" she asked.

As much as his body ached to be near Sara, part of him was angry his daughter had confided her pain to someone besides him. And he wanted her to know it. "There's only room for two on the ATVs, Hollywood."

"Einstein in a Stetson, aren't you? Thanks for pointing that out. I was thinking I'd have my own four-wheeler."

Her attitude made him grin despite himself. "You think you can handle it?"

She matched his smile. "Oh, yeah. I can handle it."

Claire cleared her throat, and Sara turned that million-watt grin on his daughter. "What do you say? I bet I can beat you and your old man to the top of the pass."

"He's knows a lot about ATVs."

Sara tossed her hair. "I'm not scared of his ego."

Claire gave a tiny giggle. "We're going to kick your butt," she said quietly.

"Oh, smack talk," Sara said with a loud laugh. "Guess the cowboy isn't the only one in the Travers family with a healthy ego. I love it. I'll help April pack a lunch while you two get the equipment ready."

Claire popped up off the bed and took two steps before Josh saw her realize her part of the deal. She slowed, dragging one bare foot across the carpet. "I guess that would be okay."

Josh didn't wait for her to change her mind. "Let's go, then," he said, hoping he sounded enthusiastic and not as scared as he was to mess up this chance with her. "We'll make sure Sara gets the slow one," he added in a stage whisper.

"Dad, that's not fair." Claire wiggled a finger at him.

"Right. Sorry."

"I mean, we're going to beat her bad enough as it is." Claire's eyes danced as she grinned at him and his heart skipped a beat. Her smile was so like his sister, Beth's. A smile he missed like he missed riding.

"You bet we are," he agreed, and motioned her to lead him out the door.

As she walked past, he met Sara's gaze. She arched a brow.

"Thank you," he mouthed.

Instead of the sassy comeback he expected, she only nodded and shooed him after Claire.

Chapter Six

"Get her!" Claire yelled in his ear over the roar of the four-wheeler's motor. "She's killing us."

Josh smiled as he hit the gas. He watched Sara's jeans stretch tight across her perfect bottom as she leaned into a turn on the narrow trail. He couldn't muster one bit of temper at getting his butt kicked by Hollywood Barbie. He was simply having too much fun racing up the mountain with his daughter's laughter filling him and her small arms wrapped around his waist as though she was totally comfortable in the moment. As though she trusted him.

He pushed hard on the throttle because the one thing Claire trusted him to do right now was catch up to Sara.

This day was another revelation about Sara. He'd expected her to be hesitant and unsure on the ATV, since she said she'd never ridden one before. But after a few minutes of instruction and warm-up, she took off on the dirt road that led from the property to the forest service trail as though she'd spent her life on the mountain.

Between the pain in his leg and Claire's extra weight behind him, it had taken Josh longer to find his groove. By that time, Sara was at least three hundred yards ahead of them.

She looked back over her shoulder, and her grin widened, hair escaping its ponytail under the helmet to whirl around her neck. He felt something unfamiliar around his stomach as he followed her, the powerful ATV vibrating under him, and realized it was happiness—an emotion he hadn't experienced in far too long.

Most of his last two years on the PBR tour had been spent defending his title and reputation from a new crop of upstarts willing to risk life and limb for a steady paycheck and an adrenaline rush. Green kids, the same as

Josh had been when he'd first gone pro, with nothing to hold him down or back in his quest for fame and what little fortune there was to be had in the arena. Years on the back of a bull had taken its toll on his mind and body. He still felt the repercussions as he maneuvered around a fallen log, his back screaming as his knee throbbed.

"We're gaining on her," Claire yelled in his ear. "Go, Dad, go! You can do it!"

A surge of power coursed through him. Who needed Advil when he had his daughter's confidence?

"Hold on tight," he answered, and took a sharp left onto a single-track trail invisible to anyone unfamiliar with this mountain.

They sped along rocks and exposed roots. Hundred-year-old pine trees rose on either side of the trail, the smell of the woods thick and warm on this beautiful afternoon. It reminded him of all the reasons he'd come here with his daughter, why he believed—with enough time and patience—this place could heal them both.

Claire let out a delighted screech and Josh's smile spread. "Almost there."

He made another turn and the forest cleared. They raced into a high country meadow, bathed in sunlight. The Rocky Mountain peaks towered in the background, their tips still covered in snow. At this altitude, Josh still felt a slight chill to the air as he slowed the ATV in the middle of the clearing.

Claire hopped off and looked around. "We did it," she screamed.

At the same moment, Sara's four-wheeler came into view. She stood up from her seat as she got closer, shock and amusement clear on her face.

Skidding to a stop in front of them, she cut the engine and sank back onto the machine, gasping for breath. "How in the world did you beat me?" she asked with a laugh.

"Shortcut," he answered simply.

Claire danced a circle around Sara's ATV. "We won, we won," she chanted, and did a complicated series of dance moves that made Josh smile.

"Nice work." Sara gave Josh a small nod as she climbed off the machine. "You did good."

Another surprise.

Josh didn't often encounter good sportsmanship, so he expected at least a little pouting or fuss. Nothing. It was like she didn't care a bit about winning. For so long Josh had been focused on competing it was hard to change gears and enjoy something just for the fun of it.

Sara seemed to appreciate his daughter's buoyant mood as much as he did. Claire wrapped her arms around her. "That was awesome!"

"It sure was." She released Claire after a long hug, and Josh watched her take in the scene in front of them. She sucked in a breath. "Wow. This is amazing."

"Yes, it is," Josh agreed, but continued to watch her.

Sensation rippled across Sara's stomach as she felt his gaze. She was careful not to look at him, afraid of what she'd see in his stormy sea eyes and what her own might reveal. She prided herself on staying in control of her emotions, and had the hard-won walls around her heart to prove it. But she'd left that self-possession somewhere on the mountain and needed a few moments to regain it.

She turned a circle to see the full meadow view, then took another deep breath and closed her eyes. Her whole body tingled from the excitement of the ride. Yep, she told herself, it was an adrenaline rush and nothing more. Not her reaction to Josh.

Not at all.

It had been years since she'd let herself go all out like she had on the mountain. She'd left the world and its troubles behind and simply felt free.

When was the last time she'd truly felt free? She honestly couldn't answer that question.

Still not trusting her emotions, she busied herself removing a backpack from the rack of the ATV. "I've got sandwiches and drinks here," she called over her shoulder.

"I'm spreading the blanket," Claire answered from the middle of the meadow.

"Is everything okay?"

Josh's voice so close to her made Sara practically leap out of her skin. "Good gravy," she said, thumping her heart with one hand. "Sneak up on a person much?"

"Avoid eye contact much?" he countered.

Sara knew a challenge when she heard it but didn't rise to the bait. "I'm trying to help out, you know, get your kid fed."

He spun her around to look at him and lifted her sunglasses onto her head. Her eyelids fluttered shut as his finger traced her eyelashes. "You left off the heavy makeup today. It's nice."

She batted at his hand. "I should have

known you'd be a sucker for plain Janes. Trust me, I won't tempt you again."

"There is nothing plain about you, Hollywood." His voice was a caress that made her insides warm and gooey. She swayed just a little. "Besides which, you tempt me each and every time I lay eyes on you. Now, tell me what's going on."

"Nothing," she said, an obvious lie. "I'm just a little light-headed, probably the altitude. Food will help."

"This is why I want the ranch to work."

She stared at him. "To make people sick?"

His mouth twitched but his eyes remained serious. "To take them out of their comfort zone," he said, dropping his arms to spread his hands wide. "These mountains change people. Inspire them. Make them see the world and their place in it in a different light. Sometimes there's no other way."

She nodded, although she didn't know if he was talking generally or about her in particular. Either way, she understood down to her soul what he meant.

"I want to do that for the people coming here. When someone books a trip with us, it's not like heading to Disney World or Fort

Lauderdale at spring break. It means something. To them. To me."

"I get it," she answered automatically, taken aback at his emotion.

"Do you? Do you understand how precious these mountains are? How few truly wild places there are left in this country? I want to celebrate that, help people appreciate it."

"A cowboy environmentalist?" Her lame attempt to lighten the moment fell flat.

He shook his head in clear frustration. "Do you think your mother's fast-talking boyfriend is going to give a rat's behind about the beauty of this place when he builds his luxury condos?"

"Rich people can have breakthroughs, too, you know."

"Not with what he has planned. Have you seen them? The plans?"

"No."

"He's going to level the trees that surround your grandmother's house. Put in a competition-size swimming pool under a huge bubble. Sure, he'll have a couple miles of paved trails—wouldn't want to scuff your running shoes on actual dirt."

"He's not going to demolish the entire forest," she argued.

"It changes things, Sara. Crimson is special. We don't need another Aspen-type playground for the rich and famous. Can't you see that?"

She did see it, but the knowledge left her in a precarious position. "What I see is that I need money and Richard Hamish has it. I haven't sold yet. You still have time, the entire season, to line up financing. But if not, you know what I have to do."

He crossed his arms over his chest. "Spoken like a true Californian."

"Was that the reason you let me come today, to prove some kind of point?" Despite her rising anger, her heart hammered in her chest anticipating his answer.

He stared at her, then sighed and said, "No. I wanted you to see this because it's amazing and breathtaking. I thought you'd like it. Both you and Claire." Reaching out, his thumb trailed across the skin exposed above the collar of her V-neck sweatshirt. "I wanted you here."

She itched for a fight, a reason to funnel her traitorous emotions into anger. She needed to pull away, from this man and his daughter, from the house that her grandmother had loved. The place that, despite her best efforts,

Sara had quickly come to consider home. The honesty of his response and the warmth in his gaze melted away her defenses, and she felt herself more drawn to him than ever.

Her hand lifted to his, her fingers rubbing his calloused palm. "Let's focus on that, okay? Just for now. Can you do that? We'll have lunch, make Claire happy and deal with the rest later."

Her own version of a peace offering.

He lifted her fingers to his mouth and rubbed his lips across her knuckles. Butterflies flitted along her spine in response. "Later," he murmured.

Somehow she didn't think he was talking about their problems.

Which scared her even more.

Sara left Josh and Claire in the equipment garage two hours later and brought the backpacks into the kitchen to clean up. The afternoon had been perfect, relaxed and easy, with dad and daughter actually having a real conversation about Claire's homesickness for her old friends. Josh had suggested setting up Skype on the office computer so Claire could stay in touch, which had made Claire happy.

Neither had brought up Claire's mother or

her dubious summer activities. The question remained what would happen once school started. But that was another issue to deal with later. And not hers, she reminded herself.

She couldn't quite wipe the grin off her face and was relieved April didn't seem to be around to ask questions about the afternoon. She bent forward to put the leftover apples back into the fridge.

"You're avoiding me."

At the sound of the voice, Sara jumped, banging her head on the top of the refrigerator. "Then take a hint, Ryan," she said, rubbing the bump.

"We need to talk." He stood, one hip hitched up on the counter, wearing a wrinkled polo shirt, cargo shorts and flip-flops.

"I don't think so." She pointed at his feet. "What kind of help can you be on a ranch wearing those?"

"I had a meeting in Aspen earlier." He raised a brow. "Besides, I saw you take off with Josh. Looks like I'm not the only one playing hooky today."

She blew out a breath. "He wanted to take Claire for a ride. It made her more comfortable if I came, too."

"You're still as much of an addict as me, Sara."

"I was in that rehab center for publicity and you know it. I am *not* an addict."

"I'm not talking drugs or alcohol. People and their problems. You're addicted to fixing other people's issues. Makes it easier to ignore your own."

"You're crazy."

"Tell me why you're here."

"Because this house belongs to me now," she said, holding tight to the refrigerator door handle but unsure why she needed the support. "I can make more money from a successful season than a bust."

"And what will you do then?"

"Repay April the money that you gambled away. Finally start the yoga center she wants."

"Her dream. Her problem."

"She's my friend, Ryan. The only one who's stuck with me all these years. And I want to run a business. I want to *do* something. Something real. Can't you get that?"

"Read for the part. That's real. Do you really think you can go back to L.A. and run an exercise studio? Cater to whatever star of the week flounces through the front door looking to use yoga as a front for her latest eating disorder?"

Her eyes narrowed. "It would sure beat waiting tables and clearing up their plates of barely touched food."

"You're an actress, Sara. It's in your blood. You have something to prove still. I know it. Don't give up on your dream."

"Acting wasn't my dream, Ryan. That one belonged to my mother." It was true, but so was his comment about Sara having something to prove. She hated that her career had fizzled so publicly. If she'd been able to walk away on her own terms, with some of her pride intact...well, maybe that would have made a difference. She didn't know. What could she do about it now? Read for a part and open herself up to more ridicule? She'd swallowed loads of that in the past and wasn't sure she could stomach any more.

"Your mother's here right now."

Her gaze flicked to Ryan's face. He looked guilty and sheepish. "Why?" she said on a growl.

"To help you. Sell this place to her boyfriend. He tells me he made you a pretty good offer."

"It's not worth what he plans to do to this

place. It was my grandmother's house, Ryan. Her home. I may not have known her well, but I have to respect what she built here. I can't let it be destroyed without at least trying to save it."

Her mind strayed to the photo album on the dresser upstairs and the genuine smile on her eight-year-old face sitting on that porch swing. She thought about the pure joy she'd felt racing through the forest earlier, the way the mountain peaks felt like they cradled this valley and the peace it brought her. A feeling she hadn't known for years, if ever.

Ryan's voice broke through her reverie. "He wants the property, Sara. He's going to get it one way or another."

"Not from me." Sara didn't have much to hold on to in her life, but that feeling of peace was worth fighting for. She wouldn't give it up. She glanced at the doorway to the family room. "Is she waiting?"

"In the office."

She released her death grip on the refrigerator, flexing her cramped fingers. "Put some decent shoes on and go find April. Whatever she's doing, I'm sure she can use some help."

Ryan's full mouth twisted. "She doesn't like me."

"Do you blame her?"

"I'm a cad. That's my deal. But women still like me. They can't help themselves. She's different."

Sara stifled a laugh. "I can't believe you just said that line out loud. This isn't the nineteenth century. *I'm a cad.* So what? You can't flirt and charm your way out of what you did to April. This time you may have to actually work at making things better." She paused. "Trust me, Ryan. It's worth it."

He scrubbed his hand over his face. "Fine. You deal with your mother. I'll face the wrath of the hippie princess."

"You're so brave." Sara patted his cheek as she passed him.

He held on to her wrist. "I really am sorry, Sara."

"I know. Now go make it better." She slipped from his grasp and walked out of the kitchen, hesitating at the doorway to the office.

Go make it better.

Could she take her own advice? Was it possible to make better all the things that were wrong in her relationship with her mother? Did she even want to try? Since her career had gotten so far off track, Sara hadn't seen

Rose often. She'd quickly tired of the never-ending litany of advice and criticism. Without the spotlight, Sara didn't have much to offer her mother. Rose was a stage mother in the worst sense of the word—Sara could give Lindsay Lohan or Brooke Shields a definite run for their money in the bad-mama department.

As awful and contentious as their relationship had become, some part of Sara still craved her mother's approval. That knowledge upset her more than anything. The fact that Rose could still send her into a tailspin with a well-chosen dig or subtle jab ate at her self-confidence before either of them spoke a word.

Laughter rang down to where she stood. Not her mother's voice. Claire. Sara took the steps two at a time but slowed in the hallway outside Claire's bedroom.

"That's right, dear," she heard her mother say. "Look over your shoulder. Just the hint of a smile. Make them want more of you."

Sara's stomach lurched. She'd listened to that same litany of advice for years. Before every Hollywood event, premier or even trip to the mall Rose had coached her on what to wear and how to carry herself. According to Rose, being an actress was a 24/7 occupation. Sara had never been allowed to be truly off. Even now she'd catch herself doing an unconscious hair toss when someone recognized her. Maybe the training had served her well, she thought, as it was the one thing that had made her hold her head high in the face of many moments of ridicule.

But that had nothing to do with Claire.

"What are you doing?" she asked, bracing one hand against the door frame.

Claire beamed at her. "Auntie Rose is giving me lessons on how to be a star." The girl breathed the word *star* with such reverence it made Sara's teeth hurt.

"Auntie Rose?" She flashed a pointed glance at her mother.

"Do you know who Claire's mother is?" Rose asked by way of an answer.

Sara nodded and tried not to roll her eyes.

"Jennifer Holmes, the supermodel," she answered anyway. "The girl has an *in*. You know how much that can help, Sara. How my fame opened doors for you."

Give me a break, Sara thought to herself. "Claire doesn't need doors opened for her, Mom. She's thirteen."

"I know it's a late start." Rose walked

around the desk and stood next to Claire, running one finger along her cheek. "But look at her bone structure. She was meant to be on screen. The camera will love her. I have a friend over at Disney. They're always looking for the next big thing." She tipped Claire's face to hers. "You could be it. Can you sing?"

"I think so," Claire said, looking dazed.

"Mom! Stop." Sara stepped forward and pulled Claire away from Rose. "She has a life here. A good, normal life. She's not going to California or anywhere with you. Leave her alone."

"Just because you crashed and burned..." her mother began.

At the same time Claire asked, "Don't you think I'm good enough?"

Sara squeezed her eyes shut and tried to block out the sharp stab of pain Rose's words caused. She focused on Claire. "Honey, of course you'd be amazing. That's not the point. It isn't all fun and glamour. It's not a good place sometimes. There are a lot of bad people in show business." She threw a glare at Rose. "People who only care about themselves."

"Maybe it would give me something in common with my mom. If I was famous she might come be with me instead of..." Her voice trailed off and she swiped under her eyes.

"Oh, Claire." Sara enveloped in her in a tight hug. "Why are you doing this?" she asked her mother over Claire's shoulder.

Rose smiled sweetly. "I came here today to talk to you about this house. Richard wants to stay in Colorado until you decide to sell. I need a something to keep me busy. Claire is a lovely girl. Maybe she's it."

Sara's throat tightened. "Leave her alone, Mom."

"You know how to get rid of me," Rose said softly, and tapped the corner of the bed where a stack of paperwork sat. "Are you ready to sign?"

Chapter Seven

Sara swallowed against the lump of regret balled in her throat. She'd spent years avoiding Rose, and now she wanted nothing more than to get rid of her mother. But not at the expense of her grandmother's dream. Selling would be simple and give her the money she desperately needed to repay April and get her own second chance.

Yet what would it cost her soul?

She'd given up on so much in her life, compromised her hopes and values to make life easier. She was done running from the hard stuff or letting other people bully her. If nothing else, being in Colorado had made her see that she could live life on her own terms. She had something to contribute. Her mother wasn't going to rob her of that so soon.

"I'm not selling, Mom. Not now. Not to Richard."

Rose's delicately arched eyebrows lifted. "Well, then—"

"And you're not spending any more time here. I want you to leave."

"This was my childhood home, Sara." Rose dabbed at the corner of one eye.

"You hated it here. Counted the moments until you could leave. I know the story by heart, so don't try to change it."

Her mother's eyes narrowed briefly. "You always were an ungrateful child," she said on a huff of breath. "Because of me you had every opportunity to succeed."

"Because of you I didn't have a childhood."

"Don't be dramatic, Serena."

"I quit being dramatic years ago, Mother. Now I'm trying for normal."

"Normal is boring."

"I'll take that, too."

Rose made a sound somewhere between a sigh and a growl. She wrapped one arm around Claire's small shoulders. "I'm so look-ing forward to getting to know you better, dear," she said, and flashed a smile at Sara. "I'll make a few calls to agents this week, then see if I can find a decent photographer to do some head shots of you. I bet the camera will love you the way it does your mother."

"That would be great."

Sara opened her mouth to argue but before she could get a word out, Josh appeared next to her. "There won't be any photographers or agents for my daughter, Ms. Wells." His voice was controlled, but Sara could see a muscle tick in his jaw.

Her mother's smile broadened. "Mr. Travers, how nice of you to join us. Have you been listening from the hallway?"

"Long enough to know this discussion is finished, ma'am. And I'd appreciate if you'd stop filling my daughter's head with your celebrity mumbo-jumbo."

"She has star potential," Rose cooed.

"I believe Sara asked you to leave."

"Daddy, don't be rude," Claire said, crossing her arms across her chest. "Sara's mom wants to help me."

"You don't need her kind of help."

Tears welled in Claire's wide eyes. "You don't understand anything," she yelled, and tore past Josh, her angry footfalls echoing from the stairs.

Rose pressed her soft pink lips together. "Well, that's unfortunate. How do you think her mother would feel about a chance at Claire making it in the big time?"

Josh felt his blood turn from boiling to ice-cold. He knew exactly how Jennifer would feel—thrilled about an opportunity to meet bigger Hollywood A-listers and score better drugs. While Claire's mother was still one of the most beautiful women in the world, she'd lately gotten more press for her partying than her photo spreads. She'd even lost her contract as the face of one of the big cosmetic companies because of her extracurricular activities.

The only saving grace was that the further she spiraled out of control, the less Jennifer took an interest in Claire. Josh planned to go back to court and file for sole custody once the ranch was stable and profitable. He didn't figure Jen would fight him, but that would change if she thought Claire was useful to her.

He took a step toward Rose. "Stay away from my daughter and out of my family's business," he commanded, not trying to hide his anger.

To her credit, the older woman didn't flinch. "It's too bad you're building your business in a house that should rightfully belong to me." She tapped one finger against her mouth, a slight smile playing at her lips. "Claire really is lovely. Plus she has a budding flair for the dramatic. I like that in a girl."

Sara moved in front of him before he could wrap his hands around Rose's birdlike throat. "Enough, Mother. The house belongs to me. I'm telling you to leave. Now."

Rose backed away, palms up. "I can take a hint, honey. But I'll be back. One way or another, mark my words."

"This isn't *The Terminator,* Mom." Sara leaned in and said softly, "Are you so desperate to keep your boyfriend that you'll stoop this low this to get what you want? I always thought you had a replacement guy waiting in the wings. I guess things get tougher as you age. How sad."

Josh watched Rose's perfectly bronzed cheeks turn a deep shade of pink. "I don't know what I did to deserve such an awful daughter," she said with a sputter. "I gave up everything for you and this is how you repay me? You were a horrible, colicky baby and a demanding child. You couldn't even make something of the career I practically gift wrapped for you. Does it make you happy to watch your own mother struggle when we both know you could help me if you wanted to? You make me sick."

He saw Sara's sharp intake of breath as Rose stormed past them both, slamming the door shut in her wake.

"Okay, then," Sara whispered after several moments, her back still to him. "That was fun and a great trip down memory lane." She said the last with a laugh that caught in her throat and turned into a strangled sob.

Josh reached for her and slowly turned her so she was facing him. His gut twisted at the tears that filled her eyes. "I'm sorry," he told her. "You don't deserve that."

She shook her head. "I'm the one who's sorry. That she's giving you so much trouble. For ideas she may have put into Claire's head." She swiped her hands across her face. "I'll do whatever it takes to make sure she doesn't corrupt Claire, Josh. She's an amazing girl. I know you only want what's best for her."

He trailed a thumb across a stray tear that

ran down her cheek. "Even if I'm an idiot about knowing how to talk to my own daughter?"

She sniffed. "All men are idiots sometimes." Holding up her fingertips, she cringed. "I can't cry anymore. My makeup is going to run all over the place."

He wrapped his hands around hers. "Why do you wear so much makeup anyway? You don't need it." As soon as the words were out, he regretted them. Jeez, maybe he should ask her if she was pregnant next or say her thighs were fat. He really was an idiot.

She stared at him for what seemed like minutes as he braced himself for an explosion. Instead, she said softly, "It makes me feel protected—like armor. People see the goop and not me. I like it that way."

The brutal honesty of her words contrasted with the stark vulnerability in her eyes. His breath caught and his cold, hard heart melted. She leveled him. He bent forward and dropped a soft kiss on each of her eyelids. Up close she smelled like cinnamon and honey, sweet and spicy at the same time.

"I see you," he whispered against her forehead.

"That's a James Cameron line," she answered, her voice not quite even. Her hands pressed against his chest as she pressed into him. "From *Avatar.*"

He smiled and brushed his mouth across hers. "You know a lot of movies."

"Uh-huh."

"And you talk too much."

"Probably. I think it's because—"

He covered her mouth with his, ran his tongue along the seam of her lips until she opened for him. Everything about her drew him closer. He savored the feel of her in his arms. His hands trailed up and down along her back, played with the soft strands of her hair. Her whole body pressed into him, and for a moment he tried to hide the evidence of his desire. Then she moaned into his mouth and he lost all coherent thought.

She pulled his shirt out of his waistband, and her long fingers were cool on his skin. "Good lord," he muttered as what was left of his brain cells took the fast train south.

He tugged at the top of her shirt and trailed kisses from her jaw down her neck and across her collarbone. Just as he moved aside her bra strap, a horn honked from the driveway below. He bolted upright. The horn blared again, this time followed by a chorus of loud whooping and slamming doors.

"Travers, where the hell are you? Let's get this party started, man!" a deep voice called.

Josh met Sara's gaze, knew his eyes were as hazy as hers. He stepped away and cursed under his breath, dug the heel of his hand into his forehead, willing his brain to start functioning again.

"Who is that?" she asked, her voice shaky as she readjusted her shirt.

He cursed again. "Our first guests."

"Your friends from the rodeo? I thought they weren't coming until next week."

"Sounds like they're early."

She blew out a breath. "Right. We can do this. I'll find April and have her whip up something for dinner. Most of the things on the itinerary can be moved up to the next few days. I'll make calls once everyone is settled. Ryan can at least put sheets on a few beds." She turned toward the door, all business.

He tugged on her arm, pulling her back against him, and wrapped his arms around her. "Are you okay?" he asked, his lips just grazing her ear.

"No, I'm freaking out. These are the first paying guests. Things have to be perfect."

"As long as we have cold beer and lots of food, they'll be fine. I mean, are *you* okay?"

She stiffened in his arms and he held her tighter. "I'm fine. I'm sorry about my mother. I'll try to control her better."

"You're not responsible for your mom. She shouldn't have said what she did to you. It will work out in the end. I'm not giving up." He paused then asked, "Are we okay?"

She wiggled until he released her. "There is no *we,* Josh."

Irritation bubbled in him. "That's funny, because I don't think I was kissing myself just now."

She threw him an eye roll over her shoulder. Her big blue eyes held none of the spark he'd seen earlier. She'd been so relaxed on the mountain, more of whom he believed she truly was. Not the guarded, fragile woman who stood before him now. "We were both upset. No big deal. It was a kiss, not a marriage proposal."

Her attitude got under his skin and he couldn't help baiting her. "Are you looking for a marriage proposal, Sara?"

"Not from you, cowboy," she answered with a scoff, but her shoulders tensed even more.

He wanted to grab her, kiss her until she

was once again soft and pliant in his arms. The horn honked for a third time and he heard a loud knocking at the front door.

Sara smoothed her fingers over her shirt-front. "Go greet your buddies. I'll get everyone moving."

"This conversation isn't finished," he told her as he headed for the stairs.

"My end of it is," he heard her say under her breath.

He smiled despite his frustration, wondering how the fact that she always had to get in the last word could be so endearing to him. He shook his head, making a mental note to start thinking with his brain rather than other parts of his anatomy.

Sara came through the back door of the main house an hour later. Music streamed into the kitchen as April appeared from the family room, two empty platters in her hand.

"You'd think those guys hadn't eaten in months," she grumbled. But Sara noticed her grin and the light in her eyes. April was at her best when she could take care of people.

"I've got the two big cabins made up. That should hold everyone. Do you need anything?"

"I've got another batch of wings ready to come out and a vat of queso dip almost heated. I'll need to run to the grocery tomorrow. We should at least make it through breakfast."

Sara glanced at the spotless counters. "Can I help clean up?"

April gave her a knowing look. "Go introduce yourself. They're rowdy but seem nice enough. Four guys and one girlfriend. Her name is Brandy. She's a looker in that farm-fresh way."

Sara took a tube of deep plum lipstick from her jeans pocket and applied a liberal layer to her mouth. "I don't want to interrupt."

"It's a party in there," April countered. "The more the merrier."

"Has he told them who I am?"

April's smile turned gentle. "I don't think so. It's not a big deal, you know. Maybe they won't recognize you."

"How old is Brandy?"

"Early twenties."

"Unless she was raised without a TV in the house, she'll know me."

"It doesn't matter."

"It doesn't matter in L.A. Much. I can blend in a little in the land of falling stars.

Especially with a new crop of beautiful losers coming through every year. But here it's just me—the only big fat failure for miles."

April took a pot holder and opened the oven to pull out a baking sheet of wings. They smelled delicious. "Did you ever consider you might be the only one who believes you're a failure?"

"My mom thinks I'm a failure," Sara said with a shrug.

"Your mom is a witch."

Sara snorted. April didn't call people names. Ever. "Whoa, there, lady. Them's fightin' words."

"Bring it," April said as she dumped the wings into an oversize basket. Her hands free, she turned and hugged Sara. "I'll take down your mother and the broom she rode in on."

"You're a Buddhist."

"I'll make an exception for her. And you. Go out there for a few minutes. Have fun tonight, Sara. You deserve it."

"What would I do without you?" Sara gave her friend one last squeeze and walked into the family room.

Josh and his four friends sat on the sofas and chairs surrounding the coffee table, filling the large room with their presence. Three of the men looked around Josh's age. The last one was so young he seemed barely out of puberty, despite having the broadest build in the group. Two were clearly brothers, both blond, tall and lanky. The third had a thick head of midnight-black hair and deep brown skin. The young one reached for another handful of chips, a shock of red hair falling over one eye. As a whole, they were tough, rangy and utterly male. Something Sara was unused to in Hollywood.

"It's enough testosterone to choke you," a voice said close to her ear.

Sara turned to see a young woman standing at her side who was as "farm fresh" as April had described. Her light brown hair was pulled back in a plastic clip and cascaded in healthy, unprocessed waves to the middle of her back. She wore little makeup other than a hint of lip gloss, and her soft denim shirt was tucked into a pair of high-waisted jeans. Actual Wranglers, if Sara guessed right.

"You must be Brandy," she said and held out her hand. "I'm—"

"Serena Wellens," the woman finished, her eyes widening.

"I go by Sara now. Sara Wells is my real name."

Brandy pumped Sara's hand at fever pace. "I loved *Just the Two of Us*. My sister and I lived for Tuesday nights."

"Thanks," Sara said weakly, her stomach beginning to churn. She braced herself for the questions about her career, her fall from stardom, her stint in rehab. She waited for criticism to cloud Brandy's gaze.

Her eyes clear, Brandy glanced around the room. "Josh said this house belonged to your grandmother."

That was it? Where was the third degree she was so used to from people she met in L.A.? She answered, "I didn't know her well, but she left it to me when she passed."

"It's a great setup and really nice of you to help Josh make it work this summer. Having a place of his own for Claire means the world to him."

Her mother's refrain from her childhood filled Sara's mind: "the world doesn't revolve around you." Based on life in Crimson, that might really be the case. Maybe outside the dysfunctional Hollywood bubble, people didn't care about her past. She wanted to keep the conversation away from her personal life so she asked, "Do you know Josh well?"

"Those four are like brothers." Brandy

nodded. "Manny and Josh started the circuit at the same time. Noah and Dan are the only ones related by blood, ten months apart. Irish twins, if you know what I mean? Noah doesn't actually ride. He does search and rescue up here in the mountains, but he's an honorary member of this crew. I've been dating Dave, the older one, for about five years."

"You don't look old enough for that."

"We met when I was sixteen at a county fair in Indiana. My dad's a big-time doctor so it about killed him that I had it bad for a bull rider. He'd expected me to follow in his med school footsteps. But I graduated high school and got a job at a preschool so I could have summers off to be with Dave."

"How'd your dad take that?"

"He was on fire for a while, but in his heart he wants me to be happy. He learned to live with it. You know how it goes."

Sara only wished that were true.

"We're getting married this fall." Brandy held out her left hand where a small diamond ring glittered on her finger.

"Congratulations. I hope you have a great life together. What about the baby-faced redhead?"

Brandy smiled. "That's Bryson. He's new

this year and the guys have taken him under their wing. He was dying to meet Josh so came with us to the ranch. I'm sorry if getting here early made extra work for you."

"It's no biggie." Sara watched Josh throw back his head and laugh at something Manny said. "He seems happy tonight."

"He seems happy here," Brandy corrected. "We weren't sure whether he'd recover from the accident."

Sara turned her attention more fully to the other woman. "I didn't realize his injuries were life threatening."

"The physical part was bad, but the worst part was losing his career and the life he'd known. He took it hard. If it wasn't for having to get things together for Claire, I'm not sure he would have made it."

Sara had assumed Josh's leg and the surgeries he'd endured to fix it had been the worst of his struggles. She knew a thing or two about losing a career and the emotional damage it could inflict. She hadn't considered she and Josh might have that in common.

"I'll introduce you." Brandy walked forward into the room, clearly expecting Sara to follow.

"You all need a chance to catch up," Sara

said, suddenly feeling out of place in her low-slung jeans, tight T-shirt and heavily made-up face. Even the streaks in her hair made her feel like an outsider. It was one thing to wear her carefully crafted mask in California, but these people were real. She felt like a huge phony.

"Come on." Brandy's smile was open and friendly. "They know me too well to be on their best behavior. Without backup, I'll be stuck judging burping contests, or worse."

Sara couldn't help but return Brandy's smile. "For a few minutes, I guess."

"Hey, y'all," Brandy announced over the music. "This is Sara. She's keeping Josh's tight buns out of trouble this summer. And she's taking care of all you yahoos while we're here. Try not to make her regret the hospitality."

Sara felt a blush rise to her cheeks as the attention turned to her. That and the mention of Josh's buns. Good gravy.

All four men jumped to attention. "Nice to meetcha," Dave said, coming around the coffee table to shake Sara's hand before draping a long arm across Brandy's shoulders. "Thanks for taking us in early."

"No wonder you look so dang happy," Noah

told Josh as he came to stand in front of Sara. "You are the prettiest thing I've seen in ages," he said to her, making her color deepen. She put out her hand but he swatted it away, instead grabbing her up in a bear hug and twirling her in a fast circle.

"Put her down," Josh ordered.

"Oh, darlin', you smell so good. Sweet as my mama's apple pie." He nuzzled his face into Sara's neck. She heard Josh growl behind him.

"I mean it, Noah. Enough."

Manny stepped in front of Josh. *"Señorita,"* he crooned, pulling Sara away from Noah's tight embrace. "You make us crazy hombres act even more loco." He took her hand, but instead of shaking it, brushed his lips across her knuckles.

"You've got to be kidding me," Josh grumbled.

"Wow," Sara whispered. She hadn't experienced anything like this in years. To be the center of attention for these men was strange and exhilarating, like the first time she'd flipped through channels and watched herself on TV. She felt strangely exposed, but not in a bad way like she had so many times in L.A.—still safe, although not quite herself. It gave her a dizzy sort of feeling.

"You guys are funny," she said with a gig-

gle, then cupped her hand over her mouth.
Sara was not a giggler by nature.

Manny released her hand as Noah stepped
forward. "I feel like I know you from somewhere. Do you have a twin sister?"

Sara's shook her head as her grin evapo-
rated. *Here it comes,* she thought.

He paused and wiggled his eyebrows.
"Then you must be the most beautiful girl
in the world," he said to a chorus of groans
from the rest of the group.

Josh gave him a quick thump on the head.
"Knock it off, bozo."

"Who died and made you boss of me?"
Noah countered, his good-ole-boy ease re-
placed with six feet of tall, angry man. Josh's
shoulders stiffened.

"It's okay," Sara said, stepping between
the two.

"Not to me," Josh answered. It felt like all
the air whooshed out of the room at the intensity of his tone.

Noah studied Josh. "Is there something
you're not telling us? You guys have a fling
going on here?"

"No," Sara and Josh answered at once. Josh
continued, "I don't want things complicated
while you're here."

"Uncomplicated," Dave said, giving Noah a soft elbow to the back. "That's us."

"Dinner," April announced in the ensuing silence.

As quick as that, the mood changed again. "I'm starving," Noah said, heading for the dining room.

"With service like this, we may never leave," Manny agreed with a wink at Sara as he passed.

When everyone else had left, Sara turned to Josh. "I know they're just joking with all of the compliments. Trying to be nice."

"Those guys don't do nice." He scrubbed one hand across his face.

She put her fingers on his arm, shocked at the tension in his corded muscles. "What's the problem?"

"Is Noah your type?"

"What?" The question took her aback.

"At first I thought it was Ryan, the slick Hollywood bit. But maybe you'd like slumming with a bad boy. Tell me, which way is it going to go?"

Sara sucked in a breath. "You are way out of line, Josh. My idea was to spend the night holed up in my cabin. Alone. But April convinced me to come out here to meet your friends. It was hard as hell since I was sure they'd give me the same once-over I get every day in L.A. then make a big deal about who I used to be. But you know what? Those guys were nice. And sweet. And funny. I don't get that a lot and would appreciate if you'd stop raining on my parade with your bad attitude."

She whirled away but he held her wrist. She wouldn't turn around but felt his heat against her back. "I'm sorry," he said finally.

"Fine. Now let go."

He didn't release her. "You deserve some-one nice, sweet and funny. You deserve some-one whole. I hope you find that man. Even if it's one of those guys. Any of them would be lucky to have you."

She looked over her shoulder and her breath caught at the stark pain in his eyes. "What do you mean *whole?*"

He dropped her arm. "Never mind. Let's go eat." He moved past her without another word.

As he walked from the room, her gaze caught on the slight limp in his gait that be-came more pronounced at the end of a long day. She couldn't answer for herself, but she was certain he didn't deserve the self-inflicted solitude he seemed to carry as his burden. He'd had everything in his life taken from him. Not the slow unraveling that marked her failure, but one instant that stole his future and challenged a reputation he'd built for years.

At least she knew that she could go back to acting if given the chance. His days on the back of a bull were done. She couldn't imagine the strength it had taken him to move on, to start over on the ranch and with Claire. How could he think he was anything less than whole? His strength of character was deeper than most of the men she'd known combined.

The question remained: What did she want in a man? Her eyes roved over his strong body as he disappeared around the corner, a shiver dancing along her spine. It had been years since she'd considered dating after a string of relationships with would-be actors had left her hollow inside.

Josh was 100 percent real man. As she followed him into the dining room, the thought crossed her mind that she might not even be up for the challenge that he held.

Once again, she reminded herself it was a good thing she was only on the ranch for the summer. For any number of reasons.

Chapter Eight

Josh sat through dinner with a chip on his shoulder and a pit in his stomach that prevented him from enjoying any of the delicious food April had prepared. Not so for his friends, who dug into heaping dishes of enchiladas and all the trimmings with the gusto of a pack of NFL linebackers.

What ate at his gut even more was the way Noah and Manny continued to flirt with Sara right in front of his face. Her rich, musical laughter filled the dining room as she immediately slid into the rhythm of their close circle as if she'd been a part of it for years.

That got him, too, because she was so different from any of the girls he'd met on the circuit. The ones he'd known his buddies to date throughout the years. The "buckle bunnies," as they were called, were a special brand of groupies, and it was rare to find a true love, like Dave and Brandy, when you were on the road in cheap motels and seedy diners for weeks at a time.

He took another pull on his beer and groaned inwardly when he heard the front door slam shut. One more complication for his evening.

"Daddy? Sara? Whose truck is that in the driveway?"

Claire came into the dining room, and out of the corner of his eye, Josh saw Bryson sit up straighter.

Down boy, Josh thought to himself, giving a mental eye roll at how much he sounded like an old geezer.

He got out of his chair to stand next to Claire. "Claire, I think you've met Dave and Brandy. The guy who looks like his twin is his little brother, Noah. That's Manny at the end of the table and Bryson next to him. Everyone, this is my daughter, Claire." He pointed a finger in Bryson's direction. "Off-limits," he ordered, placing a protective arm around Claire's shoulders.

"Dad," Claire said with a groan, "don't embarrass me."

"Hi, sweetie," Brandy crooned. "It's so good to see you again."

"Hey." Claire gave a small wave and shifted uncomfortably next to him. "I'll just go up to my room."

He wondered what could be wrong with Claire. There wasn't a more welcoming group than this bunch, but he got the sense that Claire was ready to bolt. Sara stood before Josh could answer. Her eyes met his for a brief second before she turned to Claire. "Did you have a good time with your friend?"

"Sure, I guess."

"Come and sit next to me. We can be newbies to this group together."

After a little push from Josh, Claire shuffled toward Sara and sank into the empty chair next to her.

Noah took up the conversation without a beat. "Did you hear about the last event?" he asked Josh.

"I don't get a lot of bull-riding news out here," Josh said without emotion. "And that's the way I—"

"It was awesome, man. I rode Big Mabel and after six seconds she really let loose. I hung on like never before, legs back and chin down just like you taught me. You wouldn't believe the high. I was in the zone like never before. You have no idea."

"I have an idea," Josh grumbled as he took his seat again.

"Five thousand dollars, dude. The biggest purse this season and it was all mine."

Manny leaned over and thumped Noah on the head. "Shut up, amigo."

"No, it's fine." Josh took another drink of his beer. "I want to hear everything." He turned to Bryson. "How's your first season going?"

Sara rubbed her hand along Claire's back as she kept one eye on Josh. "Are we still going shopping this weekend?" she asked quietly.

"Sure."

"What's wrong, honey?"

"Do you think they blame me for what happened to Dad? I mean, maybe they hate me. It was my fault he—"

"Stop," Sara said, hoping to soothe the young girl before Josh noticed her distress. "What happened to your dad wasn't your fault. We've been over this. These are his friends. I think he'd want you to enjoy tonight, not to beat yourself up."

"You're right." Claire smiled, although it looked more like a grimace.

Sara laughed softly. "That's a start." She grabbed the plate of brownies April had brought out a few minutes earlier. "Let me share something I've learned over the years. Chocolate is often the best medicine."

Claire's smile turned genuine. "I like that philosophy."

With Claire happily nibbling on the brownie, Sara turned her attention back to Josh. His full focus was on Bryson as he nodded at something the young bull rider said. To a casual observer he'd looked relaxed, but Sara noticed the tension that radiated from his jawline down through his shoulders. His fingers gripped the beer bottle with a white-knuckled grasp.

It must be so difficult for him to listen to stories from a new crop of bull riders. She knew what it was like to have failure tap you on the shoulder and ask for advice in the form of a new generation of rising stars.

Sara stood without thinking. "How about a game of charades?" Everyone at the table looked at her like she'd grown a horn. "You know, the game?" she clarified.

Continued silence and stares. Finally Dave

cleared his throat. "Cowboys don't usually play parlor games, darlin'."

Of course not. Sara felt color creep into her cheeks once again. She glanced at Josh, who'd finally loosened his grip on the beer bottle. Too bad for the cowboys, she thought. If it could keep these guys distracted and give Josh a little breathing room, she'd push them into it one way or another.

She leaned over the table toward Dave. "What's the matter? Afraid of being beat by a girl?"

Brandy gave a quiet snort of laughter. "I'm on Sara's team," she announced.

"Women against men," April added as she came into the room. "Perfect."

Josh pushed away from the table. "I don't think—"

Sara made squawking noises and flapped her elbows.

Josh's eyes widened. "Are you calling me a chicken?"

Sara smiled broadly. "If the feathers fit."

"Come on, boys," Josh ordered. "Into the family room. These ladies are begging to be trounced."

"Charades," Dave mumbled, but stood without argument. "This has to be a first."

"Should I come, too?" Claire asked.

"It wouldn't be a girls' team without you," Sara told her, meeting Josh's gaze for a brief second. She thought she saw gratitude and maybe a little relief before his mask snapped into place.

"Let's do this." He hustled the other bull riders out of the dining room, grumbling all the way.

Sara didn't make it back to her cabin until close to eleven, way past her bedtime with the early-morning hours on the ranch. She'd helped April clean up in the kitchen after Brandy and Claire had gone to bed, leaving the guys to relive old stories around the fire pit on the side patio.

To her surprise, Ryan had seemed to find his place in the overtestosteroned group, happily sharing stories of which Hollywood starlets had what body parts surgically enhanced.

She smiled to herself at the stories she could tell if she wanted, then jumped at a noise from the trees next to her front door.

"Heart-attack central over here," she squeaked as Josh stepped out of the darkness.

"Sorry." He didn't look sorry. He looked big and gorgeous in his soft flannel shirt, faded jeans and boots. A light was on in her cabin, its glow illuminating the front step enough for her to see him clearly.

Late-night stubble shadowed his jaw, defining it even more and making her wonder how that roughness would feel across her skin. She quickly pulled her mind away from that train of thought. No good could come from there.

"Expecting someone else?" he asked.

"Yogi Bear?" she answered, still trying to catch her breath. "Or Grizzly Adams, maybe?"

One corner of his mouth hitched up, matching the catch in her throat. "Noah likes you."

"I got the impression Noah likes anyone with breasts and a pulse."

That drew a laugh from him. "Probably. The question is, do you like him?"

Something in his tone of voice put her on edge. "I don't think that's any of your business." She took a step toward her door but he blocked the path.

"It is if you're going to mix business with pleasure."

She eyed him for a moment then swallowed, too tired to play games or even put up a fight. "I'm not interested in Noah."

He watched her.

"Or Manny. Or Bryson."

He continued to stare.

She huffed out a breath. "I'm not after your friends. Why do I feel like there's still a problem?"

He blinked several times then mumbled, "Thank you."

"I'm having trouble following you."

"For tonight. You made Claire feel comfortable, and I have a feeling you suggested the stupid game to do the same for me."

"Everyone had fun playing the game," she said, letting a little temper seep into her voice. "I was just keeping the guests entertained. I'm sure you can handle your own feelings."

"You're right—it wasn't stupid. We did have fun. Because of you."

The cool night air licked across her bare arms and goose bumps tickled her skin in its wake. She took another deep breath, hoping the scent of the surrounding mountains would calm her. Josh's gaze fell to her chest, which had the exact opposite effect on her jumbled emotions.

His eyes squeezed shut. "I don't know how to do this."

"Do what?"

"Want you so badly and not act on it."

She knew that feeling. "There are a lot of reasons we shouldn't be together."

He nodded but said, "Tell me why I shouldn't kiss you right now."

Every shred of rational thought dissolved from her brain. Without meaning to, she swayed a tiny bit closer to him. "I don't want to."

"You don't want to kiss me?"

"I don't want to give you a reason not to," she said on a shaky laugh.

He laced his fingers with hers and tugged her closer. With his other hand he cupped the back of her head, bringing her mouth against his. Like before, his kiss mesmerized her. Her defenses, her protective walls—everything inside her loosened and traveled south to parts of her body that hadn't been lit up for years. Those bits were glowing now as he claimed her, pulling her against him and deepening the kiss.

A shiver ran across her back and he wrapped his arms tightly around her. She snuggled into the heat that radiated from his body, losing herself in his spicy scent.

Tugging at the hem of her T-shirt, his warm hands pressed against her skin for several minutes before his fingers worked at her bra strap. *Yes, yes, yes,* her reawakened senses shouted in her head. At the same time, a trickle of unease danced across her conscience.

Darned conscience.

She didn't do casual flings. That was one of the few standards she'd held true to, both in and out of the spotlight. L.A. was filled with relationships built on nothing more than mutual attraction and soul-crushing loneliness. Sara hadn't given her body or her heart in a moment of weakness in the past. She wasn't going to let her hormones take over now. She knew how badly that could play out in the morning, and she wouldn't risk her pride, no matter how good it felt.

The silent snap of her bra opening brought her fully to her right mind.

"Stop." She wasn't sure if she'd said the word out loud until Josh's hands stilled on her waist.

He buried his face in the side of her neck. "Is this what you call a dramatic pause?" he asked, his voice ragged.

"We shouldn't do this."

"I hope you mean we should take it inside your cabin instead."

Sara gave him a small push and he immediately moved back. "I mean, the two of us is a bad idea for a lot of reasons."

"If I'd known you'd actually muster an argument, I'm not sure I would have asked the question."

"What do you want out of this summer, Josh?"

He tilted his head, massaged his thumb and index finger above his eyes. "Money," he answered simply.

"Is that all?"

"Give me a break on the twenty questions, Sara. My brain isn't firing on all cylinders right now." He sighed. "I want a future for Claire and me. I want this ranch to feel like home for her."

She nodded and tried not to admit that the truth in his words stung. She was used to not being a priority to anyone, even herself. But it still hurt to hear it out loud. "It's about Claire for you. For me it's about a second chance of a different kind."

In a way, things had been easier in California. The day-to-day struggle to make ends meet had left her little time to ponder the sad state of the rest of her life. Now that she had that time, it was up to her to protect herself. No one else was going to.

She liked to believe that her grandma would have fought for Sara if her mother hadn't made sure they never returned to Crimson. Maybe her grandmother would have been the positive role model Sara had so desperately needed.

She wanted to think that was why Gran had left her the house. An olive branch of sorts. Sara had no intention of letting it go to waste.

"I want the money and the fresh start it will give me. I'm going to get it one way or another. Even if that means…"

The lingering heat in his eyes went instantly frosty. "Even if that means crushing my future to guarantee your own."

"I want both of us to get what we want. I really do. But at the end of the summer, that might not be possible. I'm going to sell this house. I hope it's to you. I'm working to make sure that happens. But getting involved is a complication I'm not willing to risk."

"And that's what this is? A complication?"

"I don't know. I think so."

"What about Claire?"

"I'd never hurt Claire. You know that."

"She feels close to you. It will break her heart if you throw us over."

"That's not fair, Josh. Whatever happens,

I've been honest about my intentions. I'm not going to mess with you and Claire."

"Why does it feel like you already are?"

His anger felt like a slap in the face.

"You don't understand."

"Explain it to me, then." Frustration radiated off him, hitting her like rolling waves.

She opened her mouth but couldn't think of how to tell him how scared she was. How frightened her feelings for him and his daughter made her.

As she'd done so often in her life, she took the coward's way out. "It's late. We're both tired. You should go."

"That's what you want?"

No, no, no. "Yes." She stepped aside to let him pass.

He moved past her, but at the last moment, swept her into his arms and claimed her mouth in a kiss she felt all the way to her toes. When he finally released her, she stumbled back against the door of the cabin, her knees as wobbly as a newborn foal.

He didn't look any more in control than she did, but his voice was steady as he told her, "You think too much, Hollywood," before turning and disappearing back into the darkness.

Chapter Nine

Josh finished wiping down the last ATV and leaned back against the machine's front tire. Massaging his fingers against his leg, he thought about how happy everyone had looked coming back from last night's sunset ride.

The weather had been perfect for the past three days and his friends had taken full advantage, spending as much time as possible hiking, biking and fishing on the mountain. Yesterday afternoon, they'd ridden the four-wheelers up to the old mining town on the other side of the peak. He'd even convinced Claire to come along.

Things were exactly the way he'd pictured them for the summer. Except for watching Noah and Manny continue to flirt with Sara while Bryson made cow eyes at his daughter. That wasn't part of the plan.

Neither was the way his knee throbbed after several days of constant action.

The door to the equipment barn squeaked. "Josh, are you in here?"

Josh straightened as Dave shuffled into the barn. "I'm just cleaning things up a bit."

"That ride was killer today. The views from the top are definitely worth the price of admission."

"Yep." Josh rubbed the towel across the seat of one ATV. "Brandy seemed happy."

Dave snorted. "She's happy anytime I let her drive. That woman has the heaviest lead foot in history."

"I'm glad it's working out with the two of you."

"Me, too." His friend studied him. "Sara's pretty great."

"It's business, Dave. Nothing more."

"You don't look at her like it's business."

Josh flipped the towel onto the workbench and turned. "She's going to sell the house at the end of the summer and head back to L.A.

If I can't get the bank to finance me, there's a decent chance all my work will have been for nothing."

"Really?" Dave whistled under his breath. "She seems happy here. Not a Hollywood type. Have you thought about asking her to stay?"

"Why would I do that?"

"Because you're crazy about her."

"That'll pass."

"How long have I known you, Josh? More than ten years, right? We started the circuit the same season. I remember how bad things got with Jen, how hard you tried to make it work."

"Not hard enough."

"Sara isn't your ex-wife."

"Thanks for the insight. But I'm making a life for Claire. One that will keep her safe and out of trouble."

Dave's eyes widened a fraction. "This is about your sister," he whispered.

"Don't go there."

Dave ignored the warning in Josh's voice. "You'd been gone three years when Beth died. The car accident was stupid and tragic but not your fault."

"I should have been there for her," Josh argued, shaking his head. "I knew how bad things were between my parents, what kind of hell that house was to live in every day. I could take out my anger in the ring, but she didn't have that option. If I'd been around to help, maybe she wouldn't have been drinking that night. Maybe she'd have been strong enough to not get in that car."

"Not your fault," Dave repeated.

"It doesn't matter." Josh opened the barn door, letting bright light flood the sawdust floor. He stepped into the warmth and took a deep breath. "I have a chance to make things right for Claire. I'm not going to blow it."

"Part of Claire being happy is you being happy. Sara does that. Everyone can see it except you. Your daughter is a teenager. She needs a woman in her life who isn't as messed up as her mother. You don't have to do it alone."

Josh let his eyes drift closed. He'd done things alone for so long he wasn't sure if he knew another way. He saw how much Claire was drawn to Sara. More often than not he'd find her curled in the overstuffed chair in the office while Sara was on the computer.

At first he hadn't wanted his daughter to have anything to do with Hollywood Barbie. As time went on, he could see Sara's influence on Claire's behavior in good ways. Claire seemed less sullen and moody. Hell, she'd even smiled at him a couple of times— a big improvement over the start of the summer. He'd felt the change, hard as it was to admit, in himself, as well. Something about Sara gave a lift to his heart. Her unflagging energy and upbeat spirit drew him out of the fog that had become a constant in his life since the accident.

Could it be something more? She said she was leaving at the end of the summer, but he knew she was happy on the ranch. She also said she didn't do casual relationships. If he offered her something more, he might have a chance of changing her mind about the future.

Sara and Claire were leaving this morning to go shopping in Denver. He checked his watch and pulled off his work gloves, tossing them to Dave.

"Can you guys handle a day on your own?"

Dave nodded. "The plan was fishing, and Noah can get us to the best water."

"Then do me a favor and close up the barn. I've got someplace I need to be."

Sara stepped out of her cabin at the sound of a horn honking. *Not more unannounced guests,* she thought, then stopped at the sight of Josh's enormous black truck idling in front of her.

Claire opened the door and scrambled into the backseat. "Dad's coming with us," she called over her shoulder. "He's got his credit card. Woo-hoo!"

"Don't get too crazy," Josh told his daughter, then patted the seat next to him. "Are you ready?" he called to Sara.

To spend three hours next to him in the front seat? No way, no how.

"Sure." She walked toward the truck. "What made you decide to spend your afternoon shopping?"

He looked at her through aviator glasses so dark she couldn't see his eyes. "I have a couple of parts to pick up from a mechanic in north Denver. Thought we could stop by on the way to Cherry Creek."

Sara's stomach gave a lurch at the mention of the upscale shopping area. She was bound to be recognized, which had seemed bad enough with Claire, but to add Josh to the mix was almost too much. She had no control over the things complete strangers were willing to say to her, most of them embarrassing.

She hesitated, then hoisted herself into the

truck. She could handle whatever came her way, she told herself. This summer was about taking back her power, and dealing with public attention was part of that.

She glanced in the backseat, where Claire had already popped in a pair of earbuds. She gave Sara a thumbs-up and returned to mouthing the lyrics of the song from her iPod.

Buckling her seat belt, Sara turned to Josh. "I think we're set."

He continued to watch her, then lowered his glasses to the tip of his nose. "You're not wearing makeup again."

He'd noticed. Damn. Sara had put her hair in a long braid and applied just a touch of mascara and gloss, hoping to blend in more with the other shoppers and avoid recognition. She forced a casual smile. "I am, just not as much. Thought I'd give my skin a rest. A little detox for the pores, you know. I think…"

Josh's hand on her wrist stopped her nervous babble. "You look beautiful," he said softly, rubbing his thumb across her knuckles.

"Oh" was all she could manage. She looked down at his fingers the way she might eye a rattlesnake on the trail. Without thinking, she snatched her hand away and dug through her purse for her own sunglasses.

He gave a deep chuckle and switched the truck into gear. "Is country music okay?"

"Fine." Anything to fill the charged silence.

He swung onto the road and turned on the radio, drumming his fingers on the console in time with a song.

Sara kept her gaze focused on the scenery rolling by and soon lost herself in the beauty of the mountains. Driving in from California, she'd been so consumed with what she'd find that she'd given little thought to the jagged peaks that framed the interstate. Now she had time to take in the mountains that had been carved out to create this road through them. She thought about the hours of work it must have taken—the blood, sweat and tears of the men who built it. Her own life felt even more insignificant in comparison.

"It's humbling, isn't it?" Josh asked, as if reading her thoughts.

Sara blinked several times. "How did you know that's what I was thinking about?"

He pointed toward the front window. "It's hard not to, driving through here. The majesty of this place takes my breath away every time."

Sara nodded. "That's exactly right. It makes

me feel so small. But in a good way. Like nature is protecting us with its very mass. The
things that make me feel little in my life don't
seem to matter when I'm faced with this type
of beauty."

"I feel the same way," Josh answered, his
voice so soft she barely heard him.

Sara felt the warmth of his glance and
squirmed a bit in the seat. What happened to
his anger from before? Anger was clear-cut,
no questions. Not like the feelings his kind-
ness produced in her.

"Are the guys having a good time?" she
asked, hoping for an easier subject.

He smiled. "The best. Everything you
planned is perfect."

A little zing tripped along her spine. "The
questionnaire helps narrow down their interests. Your friends were easy. Anything loud,
with lots of adrenaline."

"When does the next group come in?"

"This weekend, only one day between
them and your crew. It's the family reunion.
Age range from toddlers to the patriarch in
his seventies."

"The old man who wants to catch a trout
with his great-grandson as part of his bucket
list?" Josh laughed. "No pressure on me."

"You have a gift for leading the groups, Josh. Everything will be fine."

"I hope it's enough to make it work."

She sighed. "Me, too," she answered, unsure if she was talking about the ranch or her life.

They talked easily the rest of the drive, about his life on the tour and the places he'd seen in his travels. The way he described them, those seconds in the ring reminded her of the way she felt the moment a director called, "Action," the spotlight on her with adrenaline pumping. While a scene wasn't life-or-death high stakes the way a ride on a thousand-pound animal could be, it had the same emotional letdown when it was over.

Talking to Josh made her remember how much she'd loved the actual acting part of her job if she could leave behind the baggage that crowded her life.

By the time they got to the shopping area, Sara felt relaxed. Claire's excitement about the boutiques that lined the streets was contagious to the point that she'd almost forgotten her trepidation about a public outing.

Josh dropped them along the block that looked the most interesting to Claire and went to park. Sara followed Claire into a store and to a rack of colorful sundresses near the front.

"I love this," Claire said on an excited breath, holding up a low-cut V-neck sundress with a deep back.

Sara stifled a laugh at what Josh would think of that choice. She thumbed through the dresses and pulled out two with a more modest neckline. "I think one of these would be perfect."

Claire hesitated, then put the first dress back. "The blue one is pretty."

Sara's sigh of relief was interrupted by a voice behind her. "Let me know if I can be of any help," a saleslady purred. "We're having a great summer sale on all dresses in the store."

Sara turned and met the woman's critical gaze with a bright smile. "Thanks. Are the dressing rooms in the back?"

To her surprise, the woman returned her smile. "Yes. Can I take those dresses for you?"

"The blue one," Sara answered, and released the breath she hadn't realized she was holding. Okay. That went well. One stranger down, dozens of others to go. She hated feeling so nervous and out of sorts, especially when Josh was along to watch her squirm.

Claire's squealing caught her attention.

"This one," the young girl said on a rapturous breath. Sara's grin broadened at the soft pink fabric draped across Claire's arm.

"It's beautiful," she agreed.

"What's beautiful?" Josh asked at her shoulder.

"Dad, look at this dress. I love, love, love it."

"Try it on then. Let's see how it fits."

Claire practically ran toward the dressing room. "Be right back," she called over her shoulder.

"I don't get women and shopping."

Sara turned to Josh, who looked more than uncomfortable standing between racks of feminine clothes. He adjusted the bill of his baseball cap lower on his face.

Sara studied the color that crept up his neck. "Are you blushing?" she asked, and followed his gaze. "At a mannequin wearing a bra and panties?"

"I don't blush," he argued, adjusting his cap again. "And I like to see a real woman wearing a bra and panties." His gaze raked her. "I'd like to see you in a bra and panties." He paused, then added softly, "Or out of them."

She swayed forward a fraction as her southern hemisphere revved to life. Glancing over her shoulder to make sure no one else had heard him, she pointed a finger at him. "You can't say that here. Your daughter's in the dressing room."

"I know where she is, and I can say whatever I want." His big shoulders shrugged. "I've got to think of something interesting to keep me going today. You need a distraction, too. You're wound like a top."

"I am not." She followed his gaze and quickly let go of the wad of fabric bunched in her hand, placing the dress back on its hanger and smoothing her hand over it. "What happened to your attitude from the other night?"

A Cheshire grin spread across his face. "I got a better one."

"I'm not sure this is any better. We agreed nothing will happen between us."

"You agreed." He took a step toward her, his hand brushing her bare arm. "I might buy you something to model later for me."

Sara coughed and sputtered at his brazen words. "I don't need you to buy me anything, and I'm not anyone's model."

Josh winked. "That's more like it. I like you all full of spunk."

"Okay, I'm ready," Claire called from the back of the store.

Sara narrowed her eyes as Josh walked toward the dressing rooms but couldn't quite stop herself from smiling.

He did that to her.

Their easy banter felt strangely right, and her whole body tingled at the message in his eyes when he looked at her. His attitude might be joking but his energy was intensely serious.

As she followed the sound of Claire's voice, the saleslady grabbed her arm and pulled her behind a bathing suit display. "Just a minute," she whispered, her head bobbing over the shelves to make sure they couldn't be heard. "I need to ask you something."

Here it comes, Sara thought, tension curling tight in her chest once again.

"Is that Josh Travers?" the woman asked, her eyes bright with expectation. "Are you with *the* Josh Travers?"

Sara blinked and looked over her shoulder. He had to have put the woman up to this. "*The* Josh Travers?"

The saleslady nodded. "He's the retired PBR champ, right?"

Sara racked her brain. "Professional Bull

Riders," she said, almost to herself. "Yep, that's him."

"I knew it." The woman patted her chest. "He's even hotter in person than on TV."

Sara felt her jaw drop. "Are you for real?"

"Ever since they put the tour on cable, my husband's been addicted. He grew up down in Calhan, so even though we're in the big city he's a cowboy at heart. He likes me to watch, too—makes him feel like I get him."

She leaned closer and squeezed Sara's arm. "Let me tell you, it's no chore sitting on the couch watching those gorgeous boys do their thing. Josh Travers was the best of the best. It does my heart good to see him getting around, looking so happy and in love."

Sara's mouth dropped farther. "In love? Oh, no. We work together. We're here with his daughter."

"Whatever you say," the saleswoman said with a knowing smile. "You look like a nice girl."

"Sara, where are you?" Claire's voice came from the back of the store.

"Let's see how that young lady did with her choices." The saleswoman pulled a stunned Sara toward the dressing room. All that worry and someone recognized her as Josh's girl-friend?

Unbelievable.

The rest of the afternoon was just as surreal. Sara noticed several people staring and a few pointing at her as they meandered up the tree-lined streets. Each time it happened, Josh gave her hand a gentle squeeze, told a bad joke or generally teased her to distraction.

Claire did her best to put a generous dent into Josh's credit balance, growing happier with each store they entered. Sara felt the same way but for a different reason. Away from the looming tension about the fate of the ranch, she and Josh relaxed into an easy camaraderie that made hope bubble in Sara. She hadn't felt the sensation in years: the possibility of a normal life.

She floated along on that feeling until they stopped for dinner at a quaint bistro at the edge of the shopping district.

The young man at the host desk informed them that without a reservation, the wait for a table would be over an hour. Claire gave a sigh of disappointment, as the cozy restaurant had been her first choice.

As Sara turned to scan the street for nearby options, a gray-haired woman approached her from the sidewalk. "Are you Serena Wellens? The one who used to be a movie star?"

Sara sucked in a breath, unused to hearing her failure phrased quite that way. She forced a smile. "I guess you could say I used to be Serena Wellens. And yes, I was an actress. I go by Sara now."

She waited for the criticism to come— as it always did. It was human nature, Sara thought. People loved to sit in judgment of others' lives. The explosion of the internet and media outlets made it easy to feel like you had insight into someone else's business, no matter how untrue so much of what was published could be.

Josh's warm hand pressed against the small of her back, reminding her to take a calming breath. "Is everything okay here?" he asked.

Claire came to stand beside her, grabbing hold of Sara's hand. "Let's find another place," she said, and gave Sara a small tug.

Sara glanced at Claire and leaned against Josh ever so slightly. *He and Claire have my back,* she thought. *They literally have my back.* One thing about being in L.A. that she'd hated was the feeling of being alone against the world, as though she had no one but herself to depend on. She'd never been her own best defense. April had been there, but in the past few years had gone through so many of her own troubles, Sara hadn't wanted to be a burden with her own insignificant worries.

Still she stood transfixed by the stranger in front of her, like a deer in headlights. "We should go," she whispered.

"Wait." The woman took a step forward and Josh moved even closer. "I have to thank you first. My daughter, she's in college now, but when she was younger her father and I got divorced. It was messy and she was caught in the cross fire."

"I'm sorry," Sara responded automatically.

"Jessica, that's my daughter, closed off emotionally. She'd barely even look at me. But she loved your show. So every week we'd watch together. It was the only time she'd let me sit next to her. We'd talk during commercials. I swear *Just the Two of Us* saved our relationship." The woman dabbed at her eyes. "I'm sure that sounds stupid to you but it's the truth."

Sara reached out and took the woman's hand. "It doesn't sound stupid. I'm flattered that you told me."

"So thank you. We've been following Amanda's career since the show ended. Not hard since she's everywhere these days."

"She's had an amazing career," Sara agreed woodenly.

"When are you going to make your comeback? You were a much better actress than she was on the show. I'm sure that hasn't changed."

"My life has gone in a different direction."

The woman let out a bark of laughter. "I read the tabloids but I don't believe half of it. It'll happen when you're ready. You have a natural gift. Always have."

Emotions clogged Sara's throat. "Thank you again," she whispered.

The maître d' from the restaurant peeked around Josh. "Ms. Wellens?" he asked. "The manager has found a table for you."

"I'll let you get on with your evening," the woman said, and with a last squeeze of Sara's arm, scuttled down the sidewalk.

Sara met Josh's questioning gaze. "That was different, even for me," she said, trying to make her tone casual.

He gave her a knowing nod. "Looks like Serena got us a table."

"She's good for something, at least."

Chapter Ten

Josh rubbed his hand over his face and gave a weary look around yet another store filled with racks of women's clothes. How many different shops had he been into today? More than in the past ten years if he had to guess. After eating, Claire had led them from one end of the ritzy neighborhood to the other.

She'd promised this would be the last one, and Josh couldn't be finished soon enough. His knee ached, his head pounded and all he wanted was to get out of the city and up into the mountains again. Sara had gamely kept up with Claire's boundless energy, but even she'd begun to wilt a little as she'd followed his daughter back to the fitting rooms.

He'd also noticed that in the whole day, Sara hadn't purchased one thing for herself. All of her attention remained focused on Claire's needs. He knew Claire had never had that with her own mother, and it made his heart open to Sara all the more.

"I'm not sure that's your size," a voice said next to him.

Sara stood just to the side of a rack of dresses, eyeing him with a smile.

He looked down at the soft fabric he clutched to his chest, then held up the dress. "It would look good on you," he said softly.

Her eyes sparked, whether with humor or temper he couldn't tell. "Today isn't about me."

"You haven't seen anything you want?"

"Doesn't matter." She sighed. "I don't have the money for new clothes."

He ignored the way his gut tightened at her comment. "I thought maybe Colorado wasn't trendy enough for you."

"What do you know about trendy?"

"More than I ever wanted to after today." He held the dress out. "Try it on," he coaxed, suddenly wanting to see her in something other than her chosen uniform of jeans and shapeless T-shirts.

"No point," she answered, but he thought he saw a sliver of longing in her gaze. Josh knew all about longing these days. Although he found it hard to believe, Sara had almost as many walls built up as he did. Right now, he wanted to crash through each and every one of them.

"You're right, though," he told her. "It doesn't matter what you wear. The bottom line is you're beautiful."

She took a step toward him and reached for the dress. "I'm not sure—"

"What do you think?"

He and Sara turned as Claire came from the back of the store. Josh felt his eyes widen. "I think you have thirty seconds to take that off and put on a decent outfit."

Sara's mouth dropped open as her gaze traveled up and down Claire. The saleswoman who'd followed Claire from the dressing room quickly backed away as Sara shot her a glare.

His daughter wore a skintight, black lace concoction that revealed more skin than it covered. Suddenly, he saw her not as his little girl but as a woman, one who was quickly going to rival her supermodel mother in the looks department. He had a visceral need to polish a shotgun or move to Tibet. Anything to avoid what the next few years held for him as a father.

"That's not the dress we'd picked," Sara said carefully.

Claire did a quick twirl, and he realized the dress was practically backless. He growled low under his breath. "No. Way."

"Dad," Claire whined, her bright smile turning to a pout. "Don't be a stick-in-the-mud. I saw Mom wearing something like this in a magazine last month. I want to have something she'll like when I go to visit her before school starts."

"You don't have a trip planned to see your mother," Josh argued. "And you're not going anywhere in that dress."

Claire's tiny hands came to rest on her hips. "I want to see her. I texted this morning and asked when she'd be back in New York. I could fly out next month if it works for her."

"What did she answer?"

Claire's mouth thinned, and she didn't meet his gaze. "She hasn't responded yet. But she will. You know how Mom does things last minute. I want to be ready."

"You aren't going to 'fly out' to be with

her. We're spending the summer in Colorado."

Claire shook her head. "You can't stop me."

"The hell I can't," he shot back.

"You're not the boss of me."

"I'm your father and you'll do as I say."

"She's my mom. You can't keep me from her."

He couldn't think straight with Claire in that dress, looking so grown-up and out of his control. He had to keep her safe. He'd do anything, say anything to make sure she stayed with him. "I'm not keeping you from her," he yelled. "She doesn't want—"

He broke off, knowing the words were a mistake as soon as he said them.

"Me," Claire finished on a sob. "You think she doesn't want me."

He watched his daughter's eyes fill with tears and cursed himself for being the biggest idiot on the planet. "Claire, I didn't mean—"

She shook her head. "You're wrong," she said quietly, the pain in her gaze cutting a deep hole in his heart. "I hate you. Mom is going to take me back. I know she will." She turned and ran for the fitting room, silence filling the small store.

He took a step forward, but Sara put a hand on his arm. "She needs some time."

"I can't let her be with Jennifer. Too many bad things could happen."

Sara shook her head. "Then don't push her away."

She was right, but that only fueled his frustration more. "What do you know about protecting the people you love? From what you've told me, April is the only friend you have and you lost her entire life savings. If you and your mother hadn't put thoughts of another world in Claire's head, we wouldn't be here today. She'd be on the ranch. She'd be safe." His hands balled into hard fists. "Only I can keep her safe."

Sara sucked in a breath as if he'd slapped her. He waited for her to argue, to fight back. His words were untrue, but he'd baited her on purpose. He needed a good fight right now, a way to get rid of the fear crawling through every pore, making him feel weak and defenseless.

Instead, she looked away. "I'm going to get Claire. Pull the truck out front. I think this day is done."

"Sara," he called out as she walked away. She shook her head and kept moving, leaving

Josh alone. His gaze dropped to the dress he held, a wrinkled, balled-up mess in his hands.

A lot like his life right now.

Sara followed Claire into the kitchen at the ranch three hours later. Three of the longest hours of her recent life. She was on edge down to her teeth after the tense ride back from Denver.

Claire had spent the entire time with her earbuds shoved in her ears, heaving dramatic sighs from the backseat as she furiously texted on her phone. Josh had turned the music loud, not the lulling country tunes from the morning but a pounding heavy-metal station that had only served to intensify Sara's headache.

She'd leaned her head against the cool window glass and tried to tune out everything around her. It was a trick she'd learned as a girl on set, the ability to ignore the world and crawl into her own internal life.

But with Josh's hulking presence next to her, it felt like all her other senses became more attuned to him when she closed her eyes. His clean, male scent. The hot tension curling from him. She could even sense the pattern of his breathing and wasn't surprised when she opened her eyes to see that his chest rose and fell at the same rate hers did.

Although the words he'd spoken were the truth, he'd hurt her feelings. Still, she wanted to reach out and comfort him. He was a bumbling bull in a china shop when it came to Claire, but at least he cared. That was more than Sara had ever gotten from either of her parents, and she knew how much it mattered.

She also knew, because April continually reminded her, that she was a sucker for lost causes. Maybe it was because her secret dream had always been that someone would care enough to rescue her. She gave the best parts of herself to people who couldn't return the emotion. Part of her fresh start, her second chance, had been the opportunity to finally take care of herself. To make herself whole and right so she could move forward with her dreams. If she let herself get too involved with Josh and Claire, all her careful plans could slip through her fingers.

She might, once again, be left with nothing.

Regardless, she couldn't stand to see either of them in this kind of pain.

"He didn't mean to hurt you," she said to Claire's back as the girl grabbed a bottle of water from the refrigerator.

April walked in from the family room. "How was the shopping trip? Do I get a fashion show tonight?"

Claire slammed shut the fridge door and whirled. "I'd like to burn every single piece of clothing my jerk of a dad bought today." She swiped at her cheeks, her desperate gaze swinging between Sara and April. "He's wrong, you know. My mom loves me. She's busy, but she loves me."

"I know, honey," Sara answered. "He knows it, too. You scared him in that dress."

"I looked scary?" Claire's voice rose to a squeak.

Sara pressed her palm to the girl's face, smoothing away a tear. "You looked gorgeous and grown-up. That's the scariest thing a father can face. It makes them a little crazy."

"A crazy jerk," Claire mumbled.

A door slammed at the front of the house. Claire looked around wildly. "I don't want to see his friends tonight. I don't want to see anyone."

Sara glanced at April. "Are you making dinner?"

"Everyone is going into town. Ryan made reservations."

"Ryan is entertaining a group of cowboys?"

April nodded. "He stopped by earlier, looking for you. He's adamant that you be there, too. For moral support."

"I'm staying here if Claire wants company."

April stepped forward. "I'll keep Claire company." She smiled. "I made chicken soup and an apple crisp earlier. I happen to know there's a Jane Austen marathon tonight. *Emma* and *Sense and Sensibility,* two of my favorites. Does that sound okay, Claire?"

The girl nodded then gave a tiny hiccup. "I'm going to take a shower. I'll be down when everyone else is gone."

She gave Sara a quick hug. "I had a good time with *you.* Sorry Dad ruined it for both of us."

"I enjoyed the day, no matter what."

"I'll get fresh towels for you," April said, and took Claire's hand, leading her up the back stairs.

Sara braced her hands on the counter and leaned forward, dropping her head to stretch out some of the tension in her neck.

"Now I ruined the whole day?"

She looked up as Josh filled the doorway leading to the front hall. His broad shoulders looked as tense as hers felt.

"You need to apologize," she answered.

"To Claire or to you?" He crossed his arms over his chest, his dark eyes unreadable in the shadows of the soft evening light.

"I'm not important here." She straightened, wiping an imaginary crumb from the counter. "Your daughter is."

"You're important to me," he said quietly.

"Don't do that, Josh."

"Do what?"

"Care."

He took a step forward at the same moment the back door of the house burst open.

"Come on, you two," Ryan said. "I've got the masses corralled into the Suburban. We need to make it to town before the poor vehicle implodes from the force of all that testosterone."

Sara saw his eyebrows raise as he studied both Josh and her. "Whatever's going on here can only be helped by a drink and some food. Let's go."

Before she could argue, Ryan took her hand and pulled her out into the night.

Josh emptied his second beer and set it on the table. He looked down to where Sara sat, Manny and Noah on either side of her. He made eye contact with the waitress and lifted his finger to order another round.

"Rough day with the girls?" Dave asked from his seat next to him.

"I'd rather spend an hour in the ring with the orneriest bull you can find than another minute shopping."

"Amen to that," his friend agreed. "But I sure do like the results."

Josh followed Dave's gaze to where Brandy did a quick two-step with young Bryson on the dance floor. She wore a short skirt and a colorful blouse that flowed as she spun to the music. "How do you two make it look so easy?" he grumbled.

"I'm smarter than you," his friend told him sagely. "I keep my mouth shut unless I'm giving her a compliment."

Josh's laugh turned into a coughing fit as Noah leaned in close to whisper in Sara's ear.

He started to stand but Dave cuffed him on the shoulder. "He's doing it to get a rise out of you."

"Looks more like he's trying to get a rise out of himself."

"It's freaking him out being in town again, but we wanted to make sure you were doing okay. Neither of us planned on ever coming back to Crimson until we heard you'd settled here."

"Wasn't my plan either, but I'm going to make it work."

"Have you seen Logan and Jake recently?"

Josh took a breath at the mention of his two brothers. "Jake was here for Mom's funeral a couple of years ago. We both stayed less than twenty-four hours. Long enough to hire someone to clear out the old house and get it on the market. He flew off to whatever country needed doctors again after that. Logan…well, he couldn't exactly get away at the time."

"I'm sorry, man. About a lot of things."

Josh did stand now. He wasn't ready for this conversation. "I'm going to stretch my legs while doing my best to ignore your brother."

He got his beer at the bar and tried not to watch his two so-called friends flirting with Sara. It wasn't any business of his what she did with her time, but it still grated on his nerves.

His eyes strayed to the woman next to him, or at least to her hands, which were busily building some sort of structure out of a pile of matchbooks. "That's quite a building you've got there," he said, focusing all his wayward attention on the intricate display.

The woman jumped three feet in the air at his words, the house of matchbooks crumbling onto the bar.

"Sorry," he said with a wince. "Looks like that took some time."

He saw color rise to her pale cheeks. She turned and gave him an embarrassed smile. "It's a silly pastime." Her light brown hair was pulled back into a tight bun at the back of her head. She began stacking the little cardboard boxes into neat rows. "You're Josh Travers, right?"

He nodded. "Have we met?"

She shook her head. "No, but my husband grew up here, so he's mentioned you." She glanced over her shoulder. "He told me Serena Wellens is staying with you for the summer."

"Her name is Sara Wells now," Josh said, his protective instinct kicking in. "Who is your husband?"

The woman closed her eyes for a moment as if she'd said too much. Just then a firm hand clasped Josh on the shoulder. "Travers, it's been a while. How's it hangin'?"

Josh turned to see Craig Wilder, one of his

least favorite people in all of Crimson, Colorado. Craig had been an insufferable prig as
a kid. His family was the wealthiest in town,
and they'd made sure everyone else knew it.
Craig had had no time for any of the Travers
kids, who were way below him on the social
totem pole. Since Josh had come back, not
much had changed. He knew Craig had become mayor last year, and he'd heard rumors
that he'd bought the election. But Josh hadn't
had a conversation with him for years, and he
didn't want to start now.

One more reason he kept to himself out on
the ranch.

"It's hanging fine," he said through clenched
teeth.

"I see you met my wife, Olivia." Craig
glanced at the woman. "Seriously, you aren't
making those stupid houses again, are you,
Liv?"

"No," she mumbled, and gave Josh an apol-
ogetic smile.

"I'm going to head back to the table," Josh
said quickly. "Dave and Noah are at the ranch
this week."

Craig stepped in front of him. "I hear Serena Wellens is there, too."

"She prefers Sara Wells," Olivia interjected.

Craig shot his wife a silencing glare. "You may have heard that in addition to my duties as mayor, I bought the old community-center building in town. I feel as though it's my civic duty to bring some culture back to Crimson. There are plenty of people who'd drive over from Aspen with the right incentive."

Josh took a slow pull on his beer. "You think Sara is the right incentive?"

"A D-list celebrity," Craig said with a chuckle, "is better than no celebrity at all."

Without thinking, Josh reached out and grabbed the other man by his shirtfront, pulling him close enough to see the whites of his eyes. "You're not using Sara for anything, Wilder. Don't talk to her. Don't even look at her. You were a slimeball when we were young, and I don't see that much has changed."

Craig fidgeted. then narrowed his eyes. "You're going to need the support of this town and the visitors' center to draw people to your ranch. Don't forget that."

Olivia stood and smiled at Josh. "I volunteer at the visitors' center. I'll make sure you get whatever publicity you need, Mr. Travers."

"Shut it, Liv," Craig said on a hiss of breath.

"I'll wait for you in the car," she answered, and turned away.

Josh released Craig and stared as he stomped off after his wife. He couldn't imagine all the things wrong in that marriage, but he'd meant what he said. He wouldn't let anyone use Sara for her fame. She deserved much more than that.

His eyes tracked to where she sat at the table. A man he didn't recognize sat next to her now, with Ryan standing between them, his face alight with excitement. The other man was clearly another Hollywood type. A shaggy beard covered his jaw, but his button-down shirt looked like some sort of expensive fabric. and a heavy gold Rolex flashed on his wrist.

Crimson had seen its share of wealth and fame. The town's close proximity to Aspen drew enough moneyed tourists to keep the town thriving. He'd been able to ignore them growing up and hoped that wouldn't change. The who's who wasn't the crowd he hoped to attract to the ranch—his ideal guests were people who'd appreciate the beauty and majesty of the mountains as much as he did. People who wanted a true Colorado vacation experience. But money was money, and he'd take what he could get if it meant having enough savings to buy the ranch at the end of the summer.

Watching Sara smile at Ryan and the other man made him wonder what she truly wanted. He was only guessing at the things that made her happy.

He had trouble believing all she cared about was selling her grandmother's house. Already she was an important part of his daughter's life and had captured a big part of his heart, even if he didn't want to admit it. But he couldn't blame her for wanting to reclaim her life on her own terms. He only hoped he could convince her there was room enough in it for him.

Chapter Eleven

Sara twirled the stem of the wineglass between her fingertips as she looked up at the stars dotting the Colorado night sky. It was well past midnight, but she wasn't the least bit tired.

She'd feigned a yawn when the group had gotten back from town, needing to be alone to sort out her thoughts. Her emotions were a jumble, and something about sitting under the vast expanse of stars calmed her frazzled nerves.

Footsteps echoed across the flagstone path that led from her small porch to the main house. She half expected Ryan to seek her out and thought about retreating into her cabin, unwilling to submit to his relentless pressure any more tonight.

But the way the hairs on her neck pricked as the figure drew closer made her think of beating a retreat for an entirely different reason. Instead. she remained rooted in her chair as Josh's tall figure came clearly into view.

"I saw your light on," he said simply as he hoisted one hip onto her front porch rail. Buster trotted forward out of the darkness, sniffed at her leg and plopped onto the ground.

"I couldn't sleep yet," she answered. "I have a lot on my mind."

He glanced up at the sky above them. "This is as good a place as any to work things out."

Her mouth curved into an unwilling smile at how succinctly he'd guessed her reason for being outside tonight. Still, she shivered as a sudden breeze whipped up from the creek bed behind the property.

"Your grandma loved that robe," he said as she cinched the belt of it tighter.

"I found it in her bedroom." She smoothed her fingers across the soft folds of chenille and cotton. "I hope you don't mind that I took it."

He waited until she met his gaze. "Everything in that house belongs to you, Sara. Don't forget that."

"It doesn't feel like mine." She shook her head. "You and Claire belong here, Josh."

"If I don't push her away." He repeated her words from earlier.

"Like you said, what do I know about making relationships work?" She tried to laugh but it caught in her throat. She wanted to muster the righteous anger she'd felt earlier but didn't have the energy or inclination for it.

"I'm sorry," he said softly. "I didn't mean that." He stood, walking to the edge of the porch. "It scares the hell out of me to think of Claire with her mother. Jennifer wouldn't know a maternal instinct if it bit her on the nose. Claire was an easy little girl, quiet and bent on pleasing whomever she was with at the time. Jennifer could send her off to school then shuttle her around on breaks, parading her in front of the media for a photo op before pawning her off on nannies or lackeys or whoever was available at the time. She let me have Claire more as she got older and had needs of her own. Now that Claire's on the verge of becoming a woman, I'm afraid Jen will treat her as a young protégé, using Claire to get into clubs or entice men." He ran a hand through his hair. "If I'm not there to protect her, there's no telling what could happen."

"Claire has a good head on her shoulders." Sara didn't know how to assuage his fears. "You've raised an amazing daughter and you have to trust she'll make the right decisions."

"I can't," he whispered miserably. "The stakes are too high. If I let her go…"

"You don't know—"

He whirled around. "I do know, Sara. My sister died in a car accident because I left her behind. I didn't take care of Beth, and I'm not going to make the same mistake with Claire."

She stood, wanting to reach out to him. For the first time she saw the stark pain his strength hid so well. Now it made sense to her. It was in the hard line of his jaw, the square set of his broad shoulders, the sharp pull of a mouth she knew to be soft as a butterfly kiss. All of that hid the pain and guilt he felt over his sister's death.

She knew what it was like to hide your true self so thoroughly that you almost believed the mask you wore was real. She knew the emotional risk involved in revealing the wound behind it.

"Tell me," she whispered.

He turned away again.

For a moment she thought he'd leap off the porch and disappear into the black night. When he didn't move, she came slowly toward him, wrapping her arms around his strong middle. Her cheek pressed against the back of his denim jacket. She breathed in his scent as she willed away the tension pouring off him. Willed him not to leave.

After a moment, his warm hands enveloped hers and he took a deep, shuddering breath. His muscles remained tight but he stayed with her. That was enough for now.

"Tell me," she said again. "Please."

"My father was a mean drunk," he began. "My mom, she both loved and feared him. I'm not sure which one made her stay. In the end, it didn't really matter. There were four of us kids. My brother Jake is two years older than me. When I was four, the twins were born. Beth and my other brother, Logan. My mom did what she could to keep us in line. My dad worked construction, mainly over in Aspen. The more time he spent building mansions for rich people, the more bitter he became about our tiny, run-down farmhouse. And the more bitter he became, the more he drank. Then…"

Sara laced her fingers in his. "What happened?"

"It's not an uncommon story in the mountains. As beautiful as it is up here, it's isolating, especially in the winter. Especially when there's not much work or a man can't hold a job because he's too tempted by the bottle. When we were young, my mom tried to keep us away from him when he was in a mood. That didn't always work with three boys underfoot. Beth was the only one of us he ever seemed to care about. She was shy and quiet. A hell of a lot easier to be around than the rest of us."

He squeezed her hands. "As soon as Jake and I got big enough to fight back, Dad left us alone. He'd take out that anger on Mom when we weren't around. She'd hide the bruises, but we knew. She never sent him away or thought of leaving. Said he needed her too much. More than we needed a decent life.

"Jake got a college scholarship and never looked back. I started on the circuit soon after. I sent money back to Mom when I could. Jake and I both did. But without us in the house to temper his behavior, Dad got even worse. Beth was so quiet, and Logan was a scrawny, sickly kid back then. Mom eventually kicked the jerk out, but it was too late. Beth and Logan were running wild. Beth had an older boyfriend. One night there was an accident. Beth and a group of friends had been drinking—the boyfriend was driving drunk. He hit an elk crossing the highway and…"

Sara wrapped her arms tighter around Josh's waist as he spoke. The anguish and guilt were clear in his tone.

"It wasn't your fault," she whispered.

"I left her here. I left both of them here. I was so intent on getting out, I deserted them. The twins weren't like Jake and me. They needed someone to protect them." He paused to drag in a miserable breath. "I should have protected them. If I'd been here…"

Sara unlaced her fingers from his and scooted around to stand in front of him. She took his face in her hands and tipped it down so he had to look her in the eyes. The pain she saw there tore at her heart. "That's why you want to keep Claire away from her mother."

"Claire was the same age as Beth when I left. I can't take the chance that something in my daughter could change. What if something happens and I'm not around to make it okay?"

"You should explain that to Claire." Sara drew her fingers through the soft hair along Josh's neck, wanting to relax some of his tension. "Right now she thinks you want to squash her fun. If she understood the reasons why you're protective of her, it might help."

"How can I admit that to her? I'm supposed to be the dad, the one with all the answers."

"You're the dad who loves her with your whole heart. That doesn't always mean you have the answers." Unable to resist, she reached on tiptoe and kissed the corner of his mouth. "You're human, Josh. Not a superhero. You know that, right?"

"If my injury has taught me anything, it's that I'm all too human."

"Human is good," she whispered. "Flesh and blood makes things more interesting."

His eyes darkened as a slow smile broke across his face.

"What did I say?"

"Flesh."

"And blood," she offered.

"Right now, I'm focused on the flesh." He drew his palms up her arms and across the front of the soft robe, rubbing his thumbs against her exposed collarbone. "Yours in particular."

As much as his touch made her skin tingle, she shook her head. "Will you talk to Claire?"

"Will you kiss me again if I say yes?"

"One doesn't have anything to do with the other," she argued, but leaned into him just the tiniest bit.

"I know," he agreed. "Yes, I'll talk to Claire."

She nodded. "You do look a little like a superhero, you know. Like you could handle the weight of the world because you're so strong and tough."

"You're talking movies again. You must be nervous."

She huffed out a breath. "I'm not nervous."

His eyebrows lifted in disbelief. "Anxious, then?" He lowered his head and touched his lips to the curve of her neck. "Or excited?"

He traced a path of kisses along her jaw, then whispered in her ear, "Wondering what it will be like between us?" His teeth grazed her earlobe gently.

Goose bumps rose along her heated skin. "We agreed this was a bad idea."

"I didn't agree to that." His fingers undid the knot of the robe's sash, then moved under the tank top she wore, massaging her back.

Her eyes drifted closed from the pleasure of his touch. She felt each of her arguments fade away in the riptide of desire building throughout her body. It was dangerous, she knew, because she felt more for this man than simple physical attraction. He'd wound his way into her heart with his quiet strength and deep commitment to doing the right thing. Sara hadn't had a lot of experience with men who were truly good, and she found it to be a heady thing and not easy to resist.

"I want you, Sara. From the moment you walked through the door, I've wanted you." His mouth moved to hers and she felt the smile on his lips. "If I were a superhero, the type who could fly and leap over tall buildings, you'd be my one weakness."

"Did you just make a movie reference for me?" She melted against him a bit more.

"Officially, it was a comic book reference, but you can interpret it any way you want. *If* it means you'll invite me in."

"Come in, Josh," she said as a sigh against his mouth.

A groan of pleasure escaped his lips as he lifted her into his arms and turned for the cabin.

She wrapped her legs around his lean waist as they all but crashed through the front door. His kisses became hotter and more demanding, drawing from her a need she hadn't known she could feel. Pleasure and passion banked inside her for years bubbled to the surface demanding a release.

Josh slammed shut the door then pressed her into it, balancing her weight with his own body as his tongue swept between her lips, mingling with hers in a dance that made her body ache with longing for him.

"Bedroom," he said on a moan.

"Can't wait," she answered, frantic to touch and be touched by him in this moment. Not wanting to delay her need one second more.

Her legs dropped to the floor, and she pushed against him while tugging at the hem of his T-shirt until he flung it off. The robe fell to the ground as they found their way to the couch. Her mouth went dry as he stripped off his boots and jeans, taking her hand as he sank onto the cushions.

She straddled his legs, feeling the evidence of his desire press against her. The realization his reaction was all for her gave Sara a feeling of power she savored, much as she did the warmth of his skin under her hands. She ran her fingers through the short hair on his chest and felt his stomach muscles contract when her tongue skimmed across his nipple.

His hands ravaged her hair, tugging gently until she looked up at him. "You're overdressed," he told her.

She stood and shimmied the pajama pants down past her hips. Then with a breath she lifted the tank top over her shoulders. Sara knew she had a decent figure—although in L.A. even the geriatric set had decent figures. She was well aware what a perfectly sculpted body looked like and just as aware that hers didn't fit the bill. She stood in front of him for a moment, hands held over her breasts in only her cotton panties, wishing she'd had the foresight and budget to buy something more worthy of the moment. But the way Josh's eyes darkened then sparked reminded her that this wasn't Hollywood.

Maybe a real guy wanted to be with a real woman after all.

The thought gave her confidence a boost at the same time as another layer of her heart's armor unfurled for this man.

She took a tentative step closer, and he moved forward to the edge of the sofa. He reached out and cupped her thighs, causing her to shuffle forward until her knees grazed the front of the couch. His mouth pressed against her stomach, drawing small circles of kisses as his fingertips mimicked the pattern on her legs.

Slowly, he gripped the sides of her underpants and smoothed them down until they fell in a puddle on the floor. He pulled her closer until she was once again on his lap, this time only the thin fabric of his boxers separating them.

"You're the most beautiful thing I've ever seen," he whispered as he took her breast in his mouth, loving the sensitive tip with his tongue. Her back arched against the pleasure he was giving her. He lifted then gently lowered her onto her back on the couch.

Sara felt open and vulnerable, unable to resist her desire in the moment. But when she looked into his eyes, there was something more. An answering need that had nothing to do with a physical release. It was as if he was claiming her with every kiss, every touch. Marking her body and soul as his. She'd never belonged to anyone, and the thought of giving herself now in that way both terrified and exhilarated her.

"You've got a pretty darn good superhero impression going tonight," she said, trying to ground herself with humor.

But the light in his eyes only glowed deeper. "And we haven't even started to fly."

He kissed her again and his hand moved down her bare skin to the place where her body needed him the most. His fingers found her core, stroking her center until her legs would barely hold her. Slowly, he lowered her to the sofa. His mouth found hers as his fingers continued to drive her wild with pleasure.

When she was so close to the brink she wasn't sure she could take any more, she turned her head. "Inside me," she whispered on a tortured breath. "I want you inside."

He lifted away from her for a moment, time enough to strip off his boxers and pull his wallet out of his jeans, yanking a condom wrapper from the side pocket. Sheathing himself, he covered her once more, his elbows resting above her shoulders as he cradled her face between his hands. "Open for me, Sara."

And she did, biting down on her lip as he filled her completely.

His lips found hers, soothing the place she'd just bitten with his tongue. Her arms wrapped around his shoulders, her fingernails grazing across the corded muscles in his back as he began to move. She moaned, or maybe it was him. Sara was so lost in the pleasure of how he made her feel she couldn't tell.

An intensity built in her body, a golden light filled every fiber of her being. He whispered her name over and over in a voice so full of reverence it made every inch of her tingle in response.

She gripped him tighter as the waves of pleasure washed over her and felt him shudder in response, his body releasing a desire that matched her own. After several minutes, they both stilled, Josh's face nuzzled into the crook of her neck. He kissed her softly, as if to soothe her fractured nerves and emotions.

"I've never felt..." she began, hardly able to put a sentence together. "That was..."

"Amazing, epic, mind-blowing, incredible," he supplied, kissing her once for each adjective he offered.

"All of the above," she admitted when she could form a coherent thought. "I don't know how else to describe it."

"No movie references do it justice?" He lifted his head to look into her eyes.

She saw a hint of amusement but also a question there. "This is better than the movies," she answered simply. "It's real."

He kissed her deeply again, an exclamation point at the end of her sentence, then cradled her in his strong arms.

* * *

Josh used one finger to trace the beam of moonlight that made a sliver of Sara's back gleam in the darkness. She gave a contented sigh and turned her cheek on the pillow.

"How was round two? Better than the first?" she asked, her voice a husky growl that gave him a satisfied tug low in his chest.

"We're a good fit," he answered.

She lifted her head to look at him. "In the bedroom, we're a good fit," she amended for him.

"Not bad on the sofa, either." He tried to ignore the shadow that crossed her face. He knew what she meant but wasn't ready to let reality intrude on this night quite yet.

"I still want to sell the house," she said quietly.

He groaned. "Don't tell me you think we made love so I could convince you not to sell the house."

"I just mean…"

"Because that would make me a royal jerk and you a bit of a hussy. Neither one of those is the case." He propped himself up on his elbow, his hand stilling on the curve of her waist.

"I know you've got goals for the summer and I've got—"

He held one finger up to her lips. "You're trying to pick a fight and it won't work. Tonight was amazing. That's enough. Let me wallow in my undeniable sexual prowess for a few minutes more. It's been a while, you know?"

Her head flopped back down onto the pillow. "I don't want your expectations to change."

"Have you ever been with a guy who hasn't wanted something from you after?"

She squeezed her eyes shut tight.

"Sara, answer me," he prompted.

"My track record with men isn't exactly stellar. Most people I know live their lives wanting something from others. For a while, I couldn't tell if men were interested in me or the doors I could open to parties, premieres and the like. Let's just say I had a lot less offers once my star began to fade."

"Nothing about you is faded," he said, and placed a kiss on the inside of her elbow. He felt her gaze on him but didn't look up. He was too afraid of what his own eyes might reveal.

He didn't expect to change Sara's mind

about selling her grandmother's property, but at the same time he still wanted…more. He wanted more for her and from her. He wanted her to see what he saw when he looked at her: a smart, beautiful woman who had so much to offer.

He knew what it was like to believe you were a one-trick pony. When he'd gotten hurt and realized he'd never ride competitively again, he figured he had nothing more to give anyone. The only thing he'd ever been good at in his life was bull riding. In the ring, nothing else mattered. Not his messed-up family, his sister's death, the tenuous relationship he had with his daughter. For those few seconds, his concentration had been completely focused on staying on the back of one thousand pounds of angry animal.

With that gone, he'd wondered what else he had in life. Then he'd gotten another chance with Claire and he'd realized that the time in the ring wasn't as important as he'd once thought.

What mattered was each tiny moment in life and how you lived it. He'd made up his mind to do better, both for Claire and himself. Slowly, he was coming to realize the accident had been an opportunity. A second chance to live life on his own terms.

He wanted Sara to realize that she was more than the on-screen persona created by Hollywood. She had choices and didn't have to prove her worth to anyone but herself.

"I got offered the audition."

He realized his hand had tightened on her hip when she fidgeted underneath it. His mind raced, then he remembered a moment from earlier in the night. "The bearded guy you were talking to at dinner?"

She nodded. "He's a hot director right now. Most of his work has been in television, but he's agreed to make Ryan's movie his first big-screen project."

"Congratulations," he said, unable to muster much enthusiasm for the word.

"Aren't you going to ask why he wants me to read?" Her eyes held a hint of accusation.

"I watched *Just the Two of Us*," Josh answered honestly. "Back when it was a network show and recently, too. Claire's been ordering each season online."

Sara swallowed and looked away. "I didn't know that."

"You were a good actress, Sara. You may be out of practice, but I doubt that has changed.

You had some bad luck, but it doesn't diminish your natural talent."

A lone tear dripped from the outside corner of her eye, and he brushed it away with his lips. "Why don't you seem happy about this?"

She blinked several times. "I stopped believing I had any talent," she told him. "The washed-up child star is such a familiar cliché in Hollywood. Why should I be any different?"

"Because you're an original." Josh took her chin in his fingers and turned her to face him. "You're better than they gave you credit for. You're more than Serena Wellens ever dreamed of being." He studied her for a minute, then added, "You know you don't have to prove anything to anyone? Not your mother, not the critics. Not Ryan or your former friends. Not even me."

"Thank you for saying that," she whispered. "How did you know Ryan is pushing me so hard?"

"That guy is full of bad ideas."

That coaxed a bit of a smile from her. "He knows the director, Jonathan Tramner, from a project they did a few years back. They reconnected because Jonathan has a place in Aspen. He was a fan of my show and, when he heard I was in Crimson, asked Ryan to set up a meeting."

"Which is why Ryan wanted to take us all out to dinner last night," Josh guessed.

"Yes." She shrugged. "The casting people will flip, but Jonathan wants me to read for the lead. He's only in Aspen through next week, so I'm supposed to get the script tomorrow." She glanced at the clock on the nightstand. "Later today, I guess. If I'm interested, I have to meet him at his place on Saturday."

"No way."

She drew back. "No way, what?"

"Even I've heard stories about what happens on casting couches. You're not going to his place alone."

That produced an actual laugh from her. "Trust me, I'm fairly long in the tooth by Hollywood standards. If Jonathan Tramner wanted to make a pass at an actress, he could find a more nubile victim than me."

"Trust me, you're plenty nubile." He scooped her up until she was pressed across the top of him, her long hair tickling his skin. "Are you sure this is what *you* want?"

She rested her arms across his chest, cradling her chin in her hands. "It's been so long since I had a chance to act, it's hard for me to know. But I loved it once. In the midst of all the other crazy in my life growing up, the actual work was good. I know you say I don't have anything to prove, but you're wrong. I have something to prove to myself."

He nodded, leaning up to kiss her on the tip of the nose. "I get that." His stomach burned at the thought of her back in Hollywood. Yet he couldn't blame her for taking another shot at the life she once loved.

Hell, what did he have to offer her here anyway? Running a guest ranch in a tiny mountain town couldn't compare with being on a movie set.

As if reading his thoughts, she said, "It's a long shot, and I'm still committed to making this summer work. To you and Claire."

"I'll drive you to the audition."

Her big eyes widened a fraction. "You don't have to do that."

"You're not alone here, Sara. I—"

Before he could say more, she kissed him sweetly on the mouth. "That's the nicest thing anyone has said to me in a long time."

He could hear the emotion in her voice and it pulled on his heart. He couldn't afford to give himself to this woman but couldn't seem to stop the tumult of emotions she created in him. Running his hands up her bare back, he deepened the kiss. "There's time before I need to go back to the main house," he whispered to her.

She wriggled her hips against his. "Let's make the most of it, then."

Chapter Twelve

"You're ready."

"I'll never be ready." Sara slumped her head onto the kitchen table and thumped it several times.

"I agree with April," Claire told her, scooping a spoonful of peanut butter from the jar. "We've been practicing every day for the past week. You're perfect for the part of Amelia. They'd be crazy not to hire you."

The more Sara thought about the audition, the more she was afraid Jonathan Tramner would be crazy if he actually did hire her. Yes, she'd rehearsed the lines, tapped into the emotion of the character, a single mother fighting for custody of her autistic son. Both April and Claire had read through pivotal scenes in the script with her dozens of times. But was she really ready to put herself out there in this way again?

Luckily, she hadn't had much time to ruminate over her doubts. After Josh's friends had left, the family reunion checked in, and she'd been busy arranging activities and making sure the needs of guests ranging in age from three to seventy-eight were met.

The family members were lovely, especially the grandparents. They'd been thrilled to share stories of their courtship and fifty-plus years of marriage. Although it was clear their children had heard the tales many times, they gamely listened over and over, adding funny commentary about childhood antics, long-ago vacations and good-natured sibling rivalries.

Being on set during her childhood had been the closest Sara had ever come to feeling like she had a family. During her summer hiatuses, she'd count down the days until she could get back to filming, the only time her life seemed to make sense. As she glanced up to her grandmother's warm, welcoming kitchen and her friends here supporting her, she thought maybe she didn't need a set to give her that sense of normalcy any longer.

"Get a new spoon," she said automatically to Claire as the girl began to dip her used one back into the peanut-butter jar.

Claire pulled a face but tossed her spoon into the sink. "You'll be great at the part of the overprotective mother," Claire said as she pulled a clean spoon out of a drawer. "You already sound like one half the time."

Sara stood and claimed a spoon for herself then dipped into the jar over Claire's shoulder. "What if I do get it? What if I don't? I can't decide which is scarier."

"You'll know what was meant to be when it happens," April counseled as she dried dishes from breakfast and put them away in the cabinets.

"How are we friends when you're always so darn zen?"

"It's the yoga," Claire told her. "You should do it with us in the morning."

"I need my beauty rest more than I need to turn my body into a pretzel." She met April's gaze over Claire's head and felt a blush creep up her cheeks at her friend's raised eyebrows.

April had been leading 7:00 a.m. yoga sessions for the guests to start each day. Sara would normally be a part of each one. Now, thanks to Josh, the early mornings after he left her cabin were the only rest she was getting. Maybe he wasn't turning her body into a pretzel each night, but she was certainly moving in ways she hadn't for a long, long time. She thought they'd been discreet about their relationship, but from the look on April's face, her friend knew exactly what was going on.

"Have you and your dad made things right?" she asked Claire, wanting to turn the attention away from April's inquisitive gaze.

"I guess," Claire mumbled around a mouthful of peanut butter. "I'm mainly ignoring him. It's easy because he's so busy with the guests."

"You need to talk to him." She wrapped one arm around Claire's small shoulders. "He loves you, sweetie."

"Your mom came by the other day," Claire countered.

Sara heard April cough to cover a laugh. The girl was young but she was good. "Yes, I know. She texted me later."

"She said there's a photographer in Aspen who does great head shots of models and actresses. She offered to drive me over."

"Your father isn't going to allow that."

Claire shrugged out of Sara's embrace. "What if I don't tell him?"

"Then I will," Sara said, her eyes narrowed. "Trust me, my mother is not someone you want in your life."

"She seems nice and she believes in me," Claire grumbled. "It's about time someone did."

"Your father believes in you. He wants to keep you safe so you have a decent future. You have choices, Claire. You can be who-ever you want."

"As long as I do exactly what my dad says. How is that a choice?"

"Talk to him. Tell him how you feel."

Claire swiped a hand across her cheek. "He doesn't care about how I feel. He wants me to be the no-trouble little girl I used to be, playing quietly with my dolls in the corner. It stinks to get older."

"Amen, sister," Sara whispered, then caught herself. "You're barely a teenager. This is new territory for both of you. I know your dad loves you. Even if he's stumbling around how he shows it."

Buster galloped into the room and nudged his big head under Claire's arm. Her eyes widened and she shook her head. "I'm crying and Dad's here. I don't want him to see me like this."

Sara took hold of her arm. "He knows you're upset. He is, too, Claire. He's driving me to Aspen this morning for the audition. Why don't you come with us?"

"Not a chance," Claire said, shaking off Sara's grip. "I'm going to hang out with friends all day."

"What friends? Where will you be?"

"Friends," the girl repeated. "I'll be around town." She took a step toward the back door. "You're not my mother, Sara. You don't need to act like you really care."

Before Sara could argue, Claire had run out of the house, Buster following close on her heels.

Josh walked into the kitchen at that moment, his gaze swinging between Sara and April. "What's going on in here?" he asked, brow furrowed.

"Hormones," both women said at once.

Josh took a step back. "Should I wait for you in the car?"

Sara shook her head. "It's Claire. I pushed her to talk to you. Probably too far." She pointed a finger at Josh. "Why haven't you made things right with her yet?"

He threw up his hands. "I've tried. She locks herself in her room anytime she's in the house and tells me she has a headache. With guests coming and going, I've barely had time to take a breath, let alone pin her down."

"It's important, Josh."

"I know."

"Maybe you should stay here instead of going to Aspen with me. Rent a bunch of vintage John Hughes movies. Anything with Molly Ringwald. Might give you a sense of what you're dealing with."

"Your audition is important, too." His brows knit in frustration. "And there's no way in hell I'm watching teeny-bopper flicks from the eighties."

Sara bit down on her lip. "I can manage the audition." She didn't want to admit how embarrassed she'd be if she bombed the read-through. The thought of Josh seeing her at her most vulnerable made her chest tighten.

"Let him take you," April told her, sliding one arm around Sara's shoulders. "You're not alone, Sara."

Sara glanced at her friend, the one who'd been at her side through both her slow de-scent into obscurity and self-sabotaging attempts to ruin her own life. April had stayed with her no matter what. There was no one Sara trusted more.

"Am I good enough?" she whispered, too desperate for the answer to care that Josh could hear her pathetic question.

"You're better," April assured her. She turned to Josh. "I'll be at the house all day, so I can keep an eye on Claire. I'll suggest that her friends come here to hang out."

"Thanks," Josh said gruffly. "I have a van coming to pick up the family reunion for the airport later this morning. We have a couple of days until the next guests arrive." He glanced at Sara. "I'll take Claire out on the ATVs tomorrow, spend the whole day with her on the mountain." He took a breath, then added, "I'll make things right."

Sara nodded. "Good. Then let's get this over with."

With a last hug for April, she made her way to the front of the house and Josh's truck. She put her hand on the door but before she could open it, Josh spun her to face him.

His lips met hers, and he kissed her for several moments, his palms encircling her face. His touch helped to melt away the anxiety she'd felt since the morning, giving her a sense of delicious pleasure that curled her toes.

"Not here," she told him when she finally broke the connection. "Claire could see us. Anyone could see us."

"I don't care," he answered, and kissed her again. "We shouldn't have to hide." He dipped his head until his eyes were level with hers. "Never think for a minute that you're not good enough, Sara."

Her gaze dropped to the ground, but he tipped up her chin until she met his eyes again. "That director would be lucky to have you on his movie, just like we're lucky to have you at the ranch. You have a place here. No matter what happens. This is your grandmother's house and it belongs to you. You belong."

A light breeze blew in from the hills behind the ranch. The swirling gray clouds in the sky matched her tumultuous emotions. As much as she didn't appreciate it when she'd first come to Colorado, the crisp scent of pines in the air had become a salve to her frazzled nerves. In more ways than one, she was acclimating to life in this small town. The very thought scared her to her core. She'd never had a true home before and wondered if she was made to last in a place like Crimson.

She bit down on her lip and nodded. "Thank you" was all she could say in response.

He opened the door and she climbed into the truck, emotion welling in her throat. Raindrops began hitting the windshield, large drops of wetness that turned into a deluge by the time he was at the end of the driveway. He didn't say anything more as they pulled out onto the two-lane highway that led to Aspen. Sara was grateful. She wasn't sure she could manage a single word right now without bursting into tears.

The sound of the rain lulled her into a quiet trance. The sudden storm was so heavy, Sara could barely see beyond the rain-soaked windows to the valley beyond. Was this a good omen? Mother Nature washing away all the old gunk she harbored? Or a bad one, the mile-high version of *The Perfect Storm?*

"Are we going to make it?" she asked, only half kidding as the rain turned to hail. A ferocious rhythm pounded outside, echoing in the truck's interior.

"A normal summer storm, that's all," Josh answered with a wink. "To make sure I'm paying attention."

She closed her eyes as he took her hand in his, soothing her with his gentle touch. It was dangerous to have her emotions this close to the surface before she went into an audition. She needed to stay professional. She concentrated on breathing, pulling air in and out of her lungs as she thought about the character she was reading for, what made the single mother tick and how Sara could use her own experience to enhance the lines she read as Amelia.

After a few minutes, her mind cleared and all that was left was the character. This was the part she loved about acting, pushing off reality and turning herself into someone new.

By the time they wound their way into downtown Aspen a half hour later, she was in the zone, despite the continuing rain. Jonathan Tramner was staying at one of the upscale boutique hotels just off the town's center. Josh pulled the truck to a stop under the building's front canopy, ignoring the valet who came around the vehicle.

"I don't want to hover like a helicopter parent today," he said with a sheepish smile. "I'm learning something from my time with Claire."

Sara turned and gave him a small smile in return. "Thank you for bringing me here. I'll go up to the audition on my own. I need to do that. Dust off my Serena Wellens attitude in the elevator."

"Leave Serena behind, sweetheart. You don't need her anymore." Josh lifted the hand he still held to his mouth, grazing a long kiss across her knuckles. "I have some things to pick up at the hardware store just outside of town. I'll be back in thirty minutes and waiting in the lobby."

She grimaced. "Are you sure you want to come back so soon? These things can sometimes take a while."

"I'll be waiting," he assured her. "And don't forget, you've got this."

I've got this, Josh thought to himself more than an hour later as he shifted in the overstuffed chair at the side of the hotel's lobby, where he was out of the way but still able to see the bank of elevators in the back. He'd thought about heading to the bar, but since it was only noon and he still had to drive back to Crimson, that didn't seem like the best idea.

He picked up his cell phone and gave it a hard shake, but the screen remained dark. Thanks to his nerves, he'd spilled an entire cup of coffee on the damn thing shortly after dropping Sara off earlier. He wasn't sure whether he was more nervous that she'd get the part or she wouldn't. Either way, his heart hammered in his chest each time the elevator doors slid open.

He believed in Sara without question and hoped that whoever this *hot* Hollywood director was would be able to see what Josh did. He'd heard her rehearsing with both April and Claire over the past week, and the emotion in her voice had made a shiver roll down his spine. If she was as good as he thought, then in no time she'd have a better offer than anything he could give her. He wasn't sure what she wanted from her next chapter in life, doubted she knew herself. His heart couldn't help hoping it would somehow involve him.

His head lifted as the elevator dinged. Before the doors had opened fully, Sara bolted out. Her wild eyes scanned the room then landed on him.

"We need to go," she yelled, and motioned him toward the front entrance. "Now."

He sprang out of the chair and caught up to her within a few strides. "What happened up there? Did he do something to you?"

"Where's your phone? Why isn't it on?" she asked, not stopping to look him in the eye.

"Sara, what's the problem?" He swung her around to face him, trying to figure out why she looked so panicked. "How was the audition?"

She shook her head. "I left in the middle of it." Her hand squeezed his arm. "It's Claire. There's been an accident. We have to get to the hospital."

Josh's mind reeled like he'd taken a sucker punch to the jaw. Her words played through his head in slow motion.

Claire. Accident. Hospital.

He turned and ran through the sliding doors leading to the street. He'd parked his truck around the corner, not wanting to bother with the valet. He reached it in seconds and fumbled for his keys, his fingers shaking uncontrollably. He took a breath and steadied himself. He'd do his daughter no good if he was too crazy to get to her.

The rain had slowed to a light drizzle, and he hit the wipers to clear the windshield as he turned the key in the ignition. Sara climbed in next to him, breathing hard from following at his breakneck pace.

He pulled out onto the street, mentally calculating the route to the hospital in his head. The facility was located between the two towns, which would put him there in about twenty minutes. Fifteen without traffic. His mind saw the stretch of highway they'd drive in detail, from the tight curves to the areas where water was likely to pool after a storm. His focus was absolute, much like it had been during his bull-riding days. That had been Josh's gift in the ring. His ability to visualize the entire ride, anticipate how the animal was going to move before it did.

Control the situation.

His current life left him feeling more out of control by the day. All his well-crafted plans amounted to nothing when his daughter was in trouble.

"What happened?" he asked, his gaze remaining fixed on the road. "Is Claire okay?"

"I don't know," Sara answered, and his knuckles tightened on the steering wheel. "April said something happened at the creek. I had terrible reception in the hotel suite so the call dropped. Why didn't you pick up your phone?"

"Spilled coffee and fried it."

"She was trying to reach you for a while before she called me." He saw her glance at the phone held tightly between her fingers. "Do you want me to try her again?"

He shook his head. "We'll be there in minutes." If his head didn't explode from the pounding inside it first. Claire needed him and he couldn't be reached. Wasn't the whole point of returning to Crimson so he'd be around to keep his daughter safe?

Now the one time she needed him, he'd failed her.

Like he'd failed his sister.

Sara reached out and placed a hand on his arm. "I'm sure she'll be fine. April would call back if there was anything else to report."

"I have to get to her," he whispered, not hiding the emotion that choked his voice. "I have to know."

Sara squeezed his arm but said nothing more. Josh knew how fast the creek on the far side of his property flowed after a heavy rainstorm. The water could go from a soft trickle to a raging current within minutes. That was how it was in the mountains. He hadn't expressly warned Claire to stay away from the creek because they hadn't been getting much rain this summer. She wasn't much inclined to be outside when she didn't have to be anyway. He should have thought of it, though. His job as her father was to think of everything he could. Josh knew all too well how losing your concentration for even a moment could cost a person. It was a lesson he didn't want his daughter to learn.

Within minutes, they pulled into the hospital parking lot. He threw the truck into Park, not caring that he'd stopped in the fire lane, and headed for the entrance.

"Claire Travers," he said to the receptionist behind the desk in the E.R. lobby. "I'm her father."

The woman barely glanced from her computer screen. "Exam Two, down the hall to your right."

Sara was beside him as he raced down the hall. At the room marked Two, Josh swung open the door. His heart skipped a year's worth of beats as he saw Claire in the bed, her eyes closed. A white bandage wound around her head and her arm was casted up to the elbow.

He must have choked out a sound because she blinked and turned her head on the pillow. "Daddy," she whispered, her voice scratchy and slow.

But she'd said his name. Her eyes were focused on his. That had to be a good sign, right?

He took two steps toward the bed, then

noticed April in the chair at the corner of the room. "She's okay," the woman told him, clearly reading the panic in his expression.

"I'm fine," Claire added groggily. "Just clumsy." She must be on some heavy pain-killers.

As he got closer, Josh noticed the scratches all along her knuckles and a large bruise forming on one cheek. He clenched his jaw with a mix of worry, frustration and anger. He hadn't been there and she'd been hurt. He wanted to punch his fist into the wall, to feel a tenth of the pain she felt.

Even more, he wanted to know how to make it better. He'd not been around enough to kiss away boo-boos or mend scraped knees when she was younger. Maybe if he had, he wouldn't be so traumatized now.

He couldn't speak, couldn't move. She looked so fragile, her face pale against the white sheet. He lifted his hand then lowered it again, not sure what to do with his mixed-up emotions.

Sara took his arm and gently led him to the side of the bed, pushing him to sit next to Claire.

"What if I hurt her more?" he said through gritted teeth, making to stand again.

"You won't," Sara assured him. She moved to stand next to him and took the hand from Claire's uninjured arm, wrapping Josh's fingers around his daughter's.

He swallowed around the lump in his throat. Claire's skin was cool to the touch, and instinctively he grasped her hand tighter, rubbing his fingers back and forth until warmth began to seep into her fingertips.

"You don't have to talk, sweetheart," Sara said, soothing her thumb across Claire's forehead below the bandage. "We're so happy you're okay."

Claire gave Sara a wobbly smile then her gaze turned to Josh. "I'm sorry I worried you. I knew it was stupid to go down to the creek after such a hard rain. Some of the kids thought it would be cool." She made a tiny sound that might have been a laugh. "I could hear your voice in my head telling me not to." She coughed, wincing from the effort.

"Don't talk," Josh told her, dragging in a shaky breath. "Rest now. I'm here. You're okay." He said the words as much for his own benefit as hers.

"She slipped on a rock and went down in the creek," April said, coming to stand at the foot of the bed. "The current was pretty strong, but she held on to a branch until one of the boys she was with could drag her out. She told me they were walking to a neighbor's house." April's breath hitched. "I'm sorry, Josh. You left me in charge and this happened. I'm so sorry."

April shook her head, then turned and left the room.

"It's not her fault," Claire said, squeezing Josh's fingers. "I lied about where I was going." She coughed again.

"Hush now," Josh told her softly. "I'm not mad at April." He lifted Claire's hand and kissed the inside of her wrist. "Or you, even though I probably should be." His voice caught as he added, "I'm just so damn glad it's not worse."

He watched as Sara bent to give Claire's cheek a gentle kiss. "I'm going to find April. You get some rest, and soon we'll take you home where you belong."

As she turned to leave, Josh caught her hand. "Thank you for taking that call," he said, and leaned up to kiss her quickly on the mouth. Her cheeks immediately turned a bright shade of pink as she glanced over her shoulder at Claire, who was now watching them with an interest that belied the effect of the painkillers.

"I'll be in the hall," Sara said, and left the room.

"So the two of you…" Claire began as Sara left the room.

Josh couldn't help but return his daughter's smile. "We'll talk about that later. We'll talk about a lot of things later. Right now, do as she said and rest. I want you out of here as soon as can be arranged."

Claire took a deep breath. "I love you, Daddy," she whispered as her eyes drifted shut.

"I love you, too, Claire-Bear," Josh answered, for the first time in years using the nickname he'd given her as a young girl.

One corner of her mouth kicked up, but within moments her breathing had slowed to an even rhythm that told him she was asleep.

He sat there for several more minutes, drinking in every one of her features. In sleep, she looked more the child than a girl on the cusp of becoming a woman. If only he could keep her small, maybe he'd be able to avoid the gray hairs he could imagine sprouting at the moment. How did any father of a teenage daughter ever sleep at night?

She'd said she could hear his voice in her

head, but she'd made the bad choice anyway. That was exactly how he'd been as a teen, almost eager to thwart his mother's advice and his father's commands at every turn. He knew all about the trouble that could come from wanting to rebel against your parents. He'd seen it in each of his siblings, and had no doubt it had contributed to his sister's tragic death.

He wasn't kidding when he'd said he was going to talk to Claire later. About everything, just like Sara had originally advised. He couldn't stop Claire from making bad decisions, but if he was honest about his own feelings, maybe she'd feel freer to share hers and not act out. It was the exact opposite to the parenting strategy his own mom and dad had taken, which led him to believe it was far more sound than anything else he could try.

At this point, Josh would try anything to avoid his past from making trouble in his present life.

Chapter Thirteen

Sara tucked the covers in tight around Claire, making the girl's slim body into a tiny cocoon, then adjusted the hot water bottle she'd placed near the bottom of the bed.

"Mmm," Claire mumbled. "Feels snug as a bug."

Hours earlier at the hospital, Sara had first comforted April, convincing her friend no one blamed her for the accident. Then she'd tracked down the doctor who'd treated Claire, making sure he discussed her injuries and treatment with Josh. The doctor reassured Josh that Claire's broken wrist was the worst of her condition and she'd recover without a problem.

Josh had been both overwhelmed and terrified at Claire being hurt. That was a normal reaction for any parent, but Sara knew that part of his anxiety had to do with memories of his sister's accident. She wanted to make sure the hospital staff didn't worry him any more than was necessary.

They'd brought Claire home just before dinnertime, and Josh had insisted on carrying her from the truck up to her bedroom. She'd been too tired to text her friends, but had begged Sara and Josh to watch part of season three of *Just the Two of Us* with her.

Unable to say no when Claire was clearly so out of it, Sara had climbed onto the bed with her while Josh hooked the iPad up to the television on the dresser. He'd positioned himself on the other side of Claire, her head resting against his strong shoulder. Sara had almost flinched when her younger self appeared on screen during the opening credits.

She'd pressed her head back against the headboard and remained resolutely still so Josh wouldn't see her reaction. They'd made it through three episodes before Claire admitted to being too tired to continue. She'd complained about a chill, and Sara'd felt almost frozen herself as she heated a water bottle and took an extra quilt from the linen closet in the hall.

Thankfully, Josh had disappeared by the time she returned to Claire's room. She bent to give Claire a kiss, surprised when the girl reached out to take her hand.

"You were a cute kid," Claire said sleepily.

"Cute only takes you so far," Sara answered.

"You're even prettier now," Claire continued as if Sara hadn't spoken. "Especially since you stopped wearing so much makeup and took the streaks out of your hair."

Sara rolled her eyes at this drug-induced critique of her beauty habits. She'd heard way worse. "I don't remember much about my gran, but I think she used to say, 'Pretty is as pretty does.' That makes more sense to me now than it used to."

"I'd like to be prettier," Claire answered around a yawn.

"You're beautiful, sweetheart."

"I haven't been much in the 'pretty does' category lately. I'm going to work on that." She tugged on Sara's sleeve until Sara sat on the edge of the bed.

"I like you with my dad," she whispered.

Sara felt her mouth drop open. "It's not serious. I mean, he's great. You know I'm only here for the summer and…"

She stopped as Claire's eyes closed. The girl's fingers dropped from her arm. Sara adjusted the pillow and blankets a bit more then straightened.

Tiptoeing out of the room, she flipped off the light and closed the door behind her.

"Not serious?" a voice asked next to her ear.

Sara jumped back, her palm landing with a thump on her chest. "Eavesdrop much?"

Josh laced his fingers in hers. "Only when it counts."

Too tired to argue, she let him lead her down the stairs. "We need to talk," he said quietly as they reached the bottom step.

"I'm tired, Josh." She huffed out a breath. "If *talk* is code for *argue,* I don't have the energy for it tonight."

"It's not," he assured her. When they stepped into the kitchen, she noticed the large trestle table was set for two, delicate china plates and beautiful crystal goblets. Candlelight danced from two pillars near the center of the table.

"What's this? Where's April?"

"April was tired. We talked and she went back to her cabin." He held up his hands at her look. "It's fine, Sara. I don't blame your friend and she knows it."

"Good, because April would do anything to keep Claire safe."

"Sit down," Josh told her softly. "You haven't eaten since breakfast."

"Did April…"

"I ordered carryout from the Italian place in town. They delivered."

"I love meatballs," Sara said on a tiny sigh.

Josh smiled. "April told me they were your favorite."

She glanced at him, stunned for a moment that on a day when he'd been through so much, he'd think of her preferences. So much for her comment about not being serious. Her heart was seriously flipping in her chest.

"You didn't have to do this," she said casually, not wanting him to see how much the small gesture affected her. "I can—"

He leaned forward and kissed her before she could continue. "Let me take care of you," he said against her lips. "Just for tonight."

He held out a chair for her and she sat, biting on her lip as she looked at the spaghetti, salad and garlic bread in bowls on the table.

Josh scooped noodles, meatballs and the rest on her plate. She unfolded the delicate linen napkin before her and spread it on her lap.

"It smells delicious," she said, breathing in the tangy scent of the food.

"It tastes even better," Josh answered, serving himself generous portions of everything.

Sara cut off a chunk of meatball and brought it to her mouth. Josh was right; the food was divine. As soon as she swallowed the first bite, she realized how hungry she was. All she had at her little cabin was granola bars and an overripe banana, so she was especially grateful for this feast.

"Tell me about the audition," Josh said after a few minutes.

The meatball that had moments earlier tasted like a little piece of heaven turned dry in mouth. "I wasn't right for the part after all," she said simply.

"You left because of Claire." Josh studied her over the rim of his wineglass.

Sara didn't drink often, but she took a big gulp of her own wine to wash down the bite of food lodged in her throat. "It doesn't matter."

"You were up there for a while. Did you read at all?"

She nodded. "Jonathan was on a call for a long time when I got there. We talked about the character for a bit. I told him how I saw Amelia. We read a small piece from the script, but I couldn't concentrate because I could feel my phone vibrating in the purse at my feet. Finally, I took the call. Then I left." She lifted her hands and forced her lips into a smile. "End of story. Not a big deal."

"It is a big deal." Josh's gaze was sympathetic. "I know how hard you worked for this reading. How much you wanted it."

"Bad timing. Story of my life." Sara pushed away her plate, her stomach suddenly rolling precariously.

"Will you get another chance?" Josh leaned forward and tried to take her hand.

She folded her arms across her chest. "This *was* my other chance."

He shook his head. "That can't be the end of it. It wasn't your fault. I'll call. Ryan can call."

She tried to laugh. "Since when are you so ready to be rid of me? I didn't think you were excited about the audition in the first place."

"I'm not. But I want you to know that

you're good. Whatever the future brings, you deserve it to be on your terms. You sacrificed a lot for Claire and me today."

"I told you it wasn't a big deal."

"I know it was a very big deal." His eyes turned dark as he watched her. "A serious deal."

"Why did you kiss me in front of Claire at the hospital?"

One broad shoulder lifted. "Because I wanted to kiss you."

"Oh" was all she could manage.

He stood, his face lit by the glow of the candles. "I want to kiss you now."

"Oh," she repeated.

"Do you want it, too?"

Her heart fluttered in her chest. She nodded, and he drew her out of her chair and into his arms, his mouth melding over hers as if his lips had been expressly formed for hers.

"I know you're not staying past the end of summer," he said, drawing back to look into her eyes.

Ask me to stay, a voice whispered inside her head.

"I can't give you the life you want here."

What if all I want is you? the voice asked silently.

She focused her gaze on his mouth, not wanting him to read the emotions she knew clouded her face.

"My priority has to be Claire."

She gave a brief nod. When would Sara ever be someone's number-one priority? His comment didn't surprise her; she couldn't blame him for it. Still, a tiny pit of despair opened in a corner of her heart. She made to turn away, but Josh held her close.

"Unless we could be enough for you."

Her gaze snapped to his. She saw a flame flickering behind his eyes that stoked a thunderous wildfire in her body.

"Would you consider making Crimson your home?" he asked softly. "I want you here. With Claire and me. It's not glamorous and there's still a long way to go before the ranch is set. But you make it better. Claire loves you and I…"

Sara held her breath as she waited for the words she hadn't known she longed to hear.

After a moment Josh continued, "I think we make a good team."

I love you. I love you. I love you. The voice in her head had gone from a whisper to a full-out yell. But she didn't say those three words. She wouldn't take the chance of scaring him

away. She knew a good offer when she saw
it. It was a perk of wading through bad ones
for so many years.

"I think I might like that," she answered
carefully. Which was only part of the truth.
What she'd like was for Josh to drop to his
knees and proclaim his undying love for her.
She'd never ask for that. Sara tried never to ask
for anything, too afraid of being disappointed.

Unaware of her inner turmoil, he bent and
claimed her mouth once again. If he wasn't
actually able to say the words, his touch certainly communicated the deep feeling she
longed for from him.

This is enough, she counseled her inner
voice. More than you ever expected.

Apparently her inner voice was a bit of a
floozy, because it gave a small sigh then commanded her to concentrate on the kiss.

Which she did without hesitation.

Josh's touch was pure magic. He wrapped
his arms around her waist as her hands twined
through his thick hair. She loved being enveloped in his strength. The heat radiating from
him warmed all the cold, lonely places in her
soul.

"Upstairs," he said as his mouth grazed
her ear.

She pushed against his shoulders with her palms. "We should clean up down here. If April comes in…"

"April won't be back tonight," he assured her as a devilish gleam lit his gaze. "Which gives me a better idea for right now."

He kissed her again, and at the same time lifted the hem of her blouse up over her head.

Sara's eyes widened. "We can't. Not here."

"Why not?" His grin turned wicked. "All the guests are gone. Claire is fast asleep and the pain meds will almost guarantee she stays that way through the night. It's only us. You own this house, Sara. You can do whatever you want with it and in it."

He stepped back, and she knew he was putting the power to decide where this night went next in her hands. Sara relished the feeling of being able to control something in her life, even if it was this one moment.

Her fingers reached behind her back and unclasped the strap of her bra. She let the satin fabric drop from her arms and smiled a bit as Josh sucked a breath. Slowly, she undid each button on her jeans, using her palms to slide the material over her hips and down her legs.

"You're going to kill me," Josh said, his voice ragged.

She straightened, wearing only her bright pink panties. "There are worse ways to die," she told him, making her tone sympathetic.

His hungry gaze rolled over her from her face to her toes then came to rest on her hips. "Put me out of my misery," he whispered. "Please."

The raw desire in his eyes made her want to run into his arms. Instead, she looped a finger through the thin waistband on either side of her underpants, bending forward a little as the small piece of fabric fell in a puddle at her feet.

"Is this what you want?" she asked, coyly placing her hands on her hips.

"You have no idea how much," he answered, and ate up the distance between them in two steps.

The moment he touched her, she realized she'd either been acting or fooling herself by thinking she was in control of this situation. Her whole body tingled in anticipation of being with him.

She tugged at his shirt but he circled her wrists in his fingers. "Not yet," he breathed against her breast before taking the puckered tip in his mouth.

Her head arched back with pleasure as he pushed her arms behind her, giving him better access to her sensitive flesh. An instant later, she let out a gasp as her bottom touched the cool granite counter.

"Right where I want you," he said, and dipped his head to place a line of kisses down her belly.

"Josh, this isn't…"

The protest died on her lips as he ran his tongue along her inner thigh. "We need to be quiet," he whispered. "No noise."

Right. Claire upstairs sleeping. April in the nearest cabin. Quiet. She could do quiet.

But when he kissed the center of her being, Sara almost had to bite down on her arm to keep from crying out. The way he touched and tasted her was perfect, as if knew her body's needs better than she did. She felt the pressure build throughout her limbs, and when the release burst over her it was like the Fourth of July, New Year's and all the other holidays rolled into one. Fireworks exploded behind her eyes and a delicious tremor coursed the length of her body.

But it wasn't enough. "Need you," she said, gulping for air. "Now."

Immediately, Josh straightened and shed his shirt and cargo pants in an instant. He fumbled with the condom packet and gave a harsh laugh. "My fingers aren't working right at the moment."

She took the foil from his hands, then wrapped her fingers around his hard length, rolling the condom over his tip. When she glanced up and winked, he gathered her into his arms, lifting her to the edge of the granite as he sheathed himself in her. Her arms wound around his shoulders. She buried her face in the crook of his neck, biting down softly on his skin. He increased his rhythm, and she matched him stroke for glorious stroke until they dived off passion's cliff together. He murmured her name over and over, his warm, calloused palms stroking up and down her back.

After a few moments, they stilled, holding each other without moving. She wished she could give her heart the same release as her body, leave it blissfully content. Instead, the dumb thing continued to pound against her chest even after her breathing had slowed.

She knew the reason, even if she didn't

want to admit it. She was in love. A litany of silly movie lines rang through her tormented mind: "You had me at hello," "You've consumed me body and soul," "You make me want to be a better…" Well, maybe she'd draw the line at Jack Nicholson.

Sappy chick flicks had been her favorite before this summer. She wondered if she'd even be able to watch one again. Because she suddenly understood the sentiment behind every tear-jerking scene. Hell, if she got the chance she should audition for one of those roles. She had a wellspring of lovelorn angst to tap.

He'd asked her to stay. Said they made a great team. Wasn't that enough?

But now that she'd really felt what it was like to be head over heels in love with someone, could she settle for anything less?

"Are you okay?" Josh drew back to look at her. He placed his hand across her chest. "Your heart's beating like crazy."

"Altitude adjustment," she said dismissively, scooting out of his grasp and bending to pick up her clothes. "That was quite a workout."

He took his own T-shirt from the chair

where it had landed and pulled it over his head. "Stay with me tonight?"

Sara swallowed, then waved at the table. "We need to clean up."

"Clean up. Then stay," he told her. "At least for a few hours."

He looped his arms around her waist. "Please."

Knowing he couldn't see it, she squeezed her eyes shut tight. "You have good manners for a cowboy." She made her tone light. Perhaps she really was a decent actress.

"Is that a yes?"

She nodded, unable to resist. Was there anything he'd ask of her that she could say no to? April had always told Sara she needed to be better about guarding her heart. But when a person spent their life with little encouragement or true affection, it was hard to stand strong when a man offered her any little bit.

She'd gotten used to living on emotional crumbs. While Josh hadn't exactly baked her a cake, he was a good man. He was doing the best he could. She couldn't fault him for that.

Why not enjoy the ride, as long as it lasted?

Sara stepped into the Crimson visitors' center later that week. She'd just picked up the new brochures for the ranch from the printer and wanted to deliver them personally.

The latest guests had left for the airport that morning, and a new crop was arriving in a few days. She was taking this, her one off day, to run errands and arrange a few promotional things in town.

She tried to let April do most of the work with the locals, still not sure of the reception she'd receive. So far today, people had acted normal, no snide remarks about her career or how she didn't fit in here in the mountains. A few of the townies at the post office had asked about the ranch, appearing pleased when she told them their booking rate. Apparently, a lot of people had been rooting for Josh and her gran. It made Sara proud to be part of the ranch's success.

Ryan had been livid when she'd explained what had happened at the audition, but that wasn't her problem anymore. She'd done what she needed to in the situation. If she'd lost her best chance at regaining her career, so be it. Other than the cast on her arm, Claire had recovered nicely. Josh had taken her out for a picnic at one of the nearby waterfalls today. He'd invited Sara to come, but she knew that father and daughter needed time for themselves.

A slender woman with a severe ponytail looked up from a computer as the door jingled. Her mouth dropped open, and Sara recognized her as one of the women who'd been in the clothing store when the shopkeeper had been so rude.

"Hello," Sara said, stepping forward while ignoring the potential awkwardness of the situation. She could make a scene, but that wouldn't do anything to help the ranch. Despite her years in showbiz, Sara'd never been one to play the drama-queen card. "Who do I talk to about these brochures for Crimson Ranch?"

"I'm sorry," the woman answered immediately.

Sara waited for her to continue with, *I don't want to promote anything you're involved in.*

Instead, the woman said softly, "For that day in Feathers and Threads when you first came to town. I shouldn't have listened to Rita gossiping about you like that. I wanted to stand up to her but..."

"I'm not used to people standing up for me." *Josh had done just that,* her irritating inner voice piped up. "Don't worry about it."

"That doesn't make it right." The woman held out a thin hand. "My name is Olivia Wilder, and I hope you'll accept my apology."

Sara's first reaction was to make a sharp comeback, probably aimed at herself. Josh had told Sara she was a difficult person to compliment. That was true, she realized. She also didn't take apologies well. It felt like letting her guard down. She'd learned long ago the negative consequences that came from that.

Olivia looked sincere, however, and Sara was growing tired of the energy it took to keep the walls built up around her. "Sara Wells," she answered. "Nice to meet you. I appreciate the apology."

Olivia's face broke into a wide smile, and Sara was amazed at the transformation. When Olivia Wilder stopped looking like she'd spent the day sitting on a large stick, she was quite lovely.

"We'd be happy to display your brochures here." She shuffled through some papers on the desk. "I also have a mailing of promotional materials going to several different cities around the state and the Midwest. A few to Texas as well, since they're a big part of our tourism business." She picked up a pen and did some quick calculations. "If you can get me an extra five hundred by the beginning of next week, I'll include you in what I send out."

"That would be fantastic," Sara said, doing a mental fist pump. "Do you manage the visitors' center?"

Olivia's mouth opened and shut a few times. "Not exactly." She tucked a stray strand of hair behind her ear. "I'm an artist, a painter. My husband is the mayor, and he likes me to stay busy with activities he deems appropriate and productive."

"Huh," Sara answered slowly. "That's funny, because you seem like a grown woman fully capable of deciding how you want to spend your own time."

"Yes, well…marriage is about compromise, I guess." Olivia flashed a smile that was anything but happy.

Sara placed a stack of brochures on the desk. "If it's what you want," she said, not believing for a minute that this woman was happy being her husband's puppet. Maybe it was because Sara had spent so many years doing other people's bidding with no concern for what she wanted from life. She could smell dissatisfaction like a bloodhound.

"I've convinced him to redo the community center," Olivia said by way of an answer. "Have you seen the building on the edge of downtown?"

"The one with scaffolding covering it?"

Olivia nodded. "It's going to be great. We'll have art classes, yoga, a camp for kids and…" she paused and pressed her lips together. "There will be an auditorium with a stage. I'd like to revive Crimson's community theater group."

"I didn't know this town had a theater group," Sara said, straightening the brochures. She looked up at Olivia and did a double take at the other woman's hopeful expression. "Oh, no. You don't expect me to get involved?"

"Craig thinks…" Olivia paused. "Of course not. Why would you give your time and talent to a small-town group? I'm sure you have more important ways to spend your time."

Sara cringed. She could tell Olivia was being sincere, but the truth was Sara didn't have anything more important to occupy her time. And nowhere to go at the end of the summer where she was really needed.

Claire needed her. Josh, too, even if he couldn't admit it. He wanted her to stay. If she could prove that she fit into his life, maybe they'd really have a chance.

Despite her fear, that was what she wanted more than anything.

"I don't have much experience in live theater."

"Most of us don't have any experience at all," Olivia answered with a smile. "I'd take any advice or help you're willing to give. There's a small improv group in town, but I think we could get a lot more people involved."

Sara nodded. "I'm not sure how long I'll be staying in Crimson," she said slowly, hating how hard those words were to choke out. "I'm happy to pitch in where I can."

Olivia's smile widened. "Craig would love to meet with you about his ideas—"

"I thought you were heading things up?"

"Well, I'm doing most of the work. But Craig likes to personally handle the VIPs."

Sara choked out a laugh. "I'm a VIP?"

"Of course."

"Do you only want me for the tiny bit of name recognition I have left?" she asked, raising her eyebrows. Better to know up front if she was being used or not.

Olivia shook her head. "You're a good actress. You have experience. I want the community center to be a success. I don't exactly understand what motivates my husband. But I'm not going to use you for publicity, if that's what you're asking. And I won't let him, either."

"You're tougher than you look," Sara observed.

"You're smarter than your reputation," Olivia shot back, then clapped a hand over her mouth. "Sorry. Shouldn't have said that out loud."

"I take it as a compliment," Sara told her. "You don't strike me as a local."

"I'm from St. Louis. Craig and I met in college. This is his hometown. He has big political dreams and thought being mayor would be a good place to start." She paused, then added, "I'm not sure I fit into his plan the way he wants me to."

"I don't fit into anyone's plan," Sara answered. "I've gotten used to making my own way." She glanced at her watch. "I'm not expected back at the ranch for a few hours. Would you want to grab a bite to eat?" She bit down on her lip as she waited for Olivia to refuse. Sara didn't have any girlfriends outside of April. She'd found that once her fame died, so had her appeal as a friend.

"Really? You want to have lunch with me?" Olivia seemed shocked.

"I do." Sara realized she truly meant it. It was time to start living outside of her own doubts. "Then I think we should do a little shopping."

Olivia gave a knowing smile. "At Feathers and Threads?"

"Exactly," Sara agreed. She glanced around. "Can you leave for a bit?"

"Absolutely. It's a slow day."

"Great. It will be nice to know a friendly face in town."

They picked a Mexican place just off Main Street that Olivia said was the best. Sara noticed a few questioning looks as the mayor's wife walked in with her. Olivia ignored them, choosing a table on the crowded patio out front.

"Are you sure you don't want something a little more secluded?" Sara asked as she slid into her seat.

"Are you embarrassed to be seen with me?"

"Very funny," Sara mumbled, but one corner of her mouth curved. She felt relaxed with

Olivia, much like she did with April, and was grateful for the possibility of a new friendship.

"If you're thinking of staying in Crimson or spending any time here in the future, the town is going to have to get used to you being around. We've had our share of celebrities wander over from Aspen, so it's not too far out of the norm."

"It's silly," Sara admitted. "Being a celebrity has a way of creeping into every aspect of your life. A lot of stars claim they want their privacy but turn around and court the fame with the vacations and outings they choose. It gets to the point where you can't live with the recognition, but you don't know how to live without it."

Olivia nodded. "My father was a U.S. senator when I was younger. He loved the attention he received from everyone in our hometown when he was back there or on the campaign trail. I know it's not the same thing, but I have an idea of what you mean."

Sara breathed a little easier thinking there was someone else in town with whom she could be honest. That was a gift she hadn't received very often in recent years.

The waiter came and took their orders. Sara thought back to her last waitressing job, the latest in a long string of them. It had paid the bills, mostly, but she hadn't taken pleasure in it. She actually enjoyed the work she did on the ranch. She liked working with guests to pinpoint activities that would make their vacations perfect. She was good at coordinating and the customer-service part of it and wanted to make a difference for them. Most people who came to Crimson, Colorado, did it because they craved an adventure. Josh was well equipped to meet their needs. Sara balanced his resources by figuring out exactly what those needs were.

They made a good combination. She wondered if her gran would have been happy with Sara's contributions to the ranch and liked to think she would have been proud.

She and Olivia ate and talked. Olivia was a few years older than Sara, and her childhood had been very different from Sara's own: daughter of a prominent senator, private school then a prestigious Midwestern college. Still, they had an easy rapport, and Olivia had many kernels of wisdom to offer about fitting in in this small mountain community.

As their plates were cleared, a shadow fell over the table. "Olivia," an icy voice said.

"You didn't tell me you'd be having lunch in town with Ms. Wellens today."

Sara looked up to see a thin, blond-haired man standing just on the other side of the gate surrounding the patio. He placed a hand on Olivia's shoulder and squeezed, but the gesture didn't look at all loving.

Sara disliked him on sight and even more when she noticed Richard Hamish, her mother's land-developer boyfriend, standing next to him.

The older man tipped his cowboy hat in her direction. "Afternoon, Serena. I've been meaning to pay a visit to Rose's family home to talk to you again about that offer."

"Her name is Sara Wells," Olivia told both men, shrugging out of her husband's grasp. "This lunch wasn't planned, Craig. Sara came into the visitors' center."

"You should have called me to join you," he said with a smile that didn't reach his eyes. "Or better yet, I could have taken her to lunch. It's not very responsible for the mayor's wife to leave her post unattended. What will visitors to our town think of that kind of welcome?"

Olivia cringed and Sara plastered a smile on her face. "They'll think whoever works at the visitors' center needs to eat and maybe the town should make arrangements for better coverage."

She turned her gaze to Richard. "Don't bother coming to the ranch. It's my home now. I own it."

"For now," the cowboy said with a smirk. "I'll send you my latest offer. I have another group of developers interested in the property. I can make you a good deal, Sara." He didn't try to hide his derision. "One that can get you out of the deep financial hole you're in."

Sara grabbed her wallet and took out a wad of bills. "It was lovely meeting you, Olivia. I hope we can schedule some girl time again." She gave Craig an icy stare. "I need to get back now."

The other woman quickly stood and gave her a quick hug. "I'm sorry," she whispered.

Sara returned the hug then turned to the two men. "I hope *not* to see either of you again anytime soon."

"I'm the mayor," Craig said coolly. "You'll see me everywhere if you have plans to stick around."

"Sara doesn't stick," the cowboy put in. "That's not the Hollywood way."

We'll see about that, Sara thought to herself. But that nagging voice inside her head suddenly sounded a lot like her mother.

If you'd only tried harder. You give up too quickly. Who are you if you're not on screen?

She glanced between the cowboy's knowing gaze, the mayor's smug smile and Olivia's sympathetic eyes.

The sympathy was the worst of it. Sympathy felt a lot like pity to Sara. She couldn't stand to be the object of anyone's pity.

She hooked her purse over her shoulder and headed for the exit, unwilling to make eye contact with anyone else. Needing to get to her car, to be alone.

When she finally did, the tears came fast and furious. Years ago, she'd vowed not to let anything make her cry, but she couldn't seem to help herself. She cried for the childhood she'd never had, for the lost innocence and all of the times she'd had to swallow her pride and self-respect. For all of the times one of her mother's boyfriends had made her feel less than who she wanted to be.

For all the times she'd made herself feel even worse.

Could this town really give her the second chance at the life she craved? It was different from the future she'd planned. Yet so far, all she'd gotten from her best-laid plans was a big pile of disappointment and failure.

She loved the acting part of the job, becoming a different character, bringing to life the words on the page. She might be just as fulfilled working in a tiny community theater as she was on a TV or movie set. She'd never know whether she was good enough to make a comeback in Hollywood, but she hoped that after a while that wouldn't matter to her any longer.

She hoped life in Crimson, Colorado, would be enough.

Chapter Fourteen

A week later, Josh watched as Sara greeted each of the ranch's new guests with a warm hug. She had a way of making every person feel comfortable and welcome. It was a gift she shared with her grandmother. Part of why he'd wanted Trudy as a partner on the ranch from the beginning had been the way she put people at ease.

Josh could lead a trail ride or a hike or a four-wheeler drive over a mountain pass, but he was often awkward with casual conversation. He preferred doing to talking. Sara filled in the gaps naturally, both with the guests at the ranch and with Claire.

His relationship with Claire was on the mend, and a large part of the reason why was Sara's encouragement. Josh had some rough edges left over from his days on the circuit and Sara smoothed them, helping him to become the father his daughter needed him to be.

Tonight, Sara's blond hair hung in soft waves around her shoulders and the pale yellow shirt she wore made her eyes seem an even deeper blue. He was glad she remained mostly makeup-free. It was as if she was finally willing to let people see who she truly was instead of her carefully cultivated mask.

Josh would never admit it to her, but a small, selfish part of him was secretly relieved nothing had come of the audition. He didn't know how to compete with her former life. He understood a little bit about the lure of lights and fame. If Sara had to make a choice between her career and life on the ranch, he couldn't imagine she'd choose him. At least not yet. They needed more time for her to really see this was where she belonged.

She drew Claire forward and introduced her to the teenage son of one of the families checking in this week.

Their occupancy was full, and to celebrate, they'd decided to have a big cookout on the patio outside the main house. April had created one of her usual amazing feasts, and Sara and Claire had handled the decorations. Tiny lights glistened from strands wound through the wrought iron gate around the edge of the patio. They'd set the tables with colorful tablecloths and mason jars filled with wildflowers picked from the meadow near the pond. The mountains provided a commanding backdrop, especially now as the sky above them turned a dozen shades of orange and red. The sun was close to dipping behind the highest peak.

This was one of Josh's favorite times on the ranch. The moment when day slipped toward evening and all the colors softened while the sounds of nature became more pronounced in the shadows.

A soft country ballad played from the speakers on the porch. The lilting melody made Josh want to gather Sara in his arms and twirl her across the path from the main house to her cabin. He loved the feel of her in his arms, and though he'd given up dancing long before his knee injury, tonight seemed like the perfect time to make an exception.

As if reading his thoughts, her gaze found his through the groups of guests milling about. He watched as her breath hitched and a blush crept across her cheeks. He hoped she could read in his eyes all the wicked things he had planned for her later.

She took a step toward him, and he realized that he was happy. For the first time in... forever, Josh felt content with his life. The ache for his sister was still there, deep in his heart. His knee would never be as strong as it once was. Despite what it had taken him to get here, or maybe because of it, Josh was truly happy with his life.

Sara had a lot to do with that. He thought about the hope in her eyes when he'd asked her to stay in Crimson. She wanted more from him, more than he believed he was willing or able to give a woman.

There was no doubt in his mind that she deserved more than he could ever give her. But if she wanted him, what was holding him back from making her his? For real. Forever.

He had a sudden vision of the future. The image included a family: Claire, Sara and maybe even a baby. One with Sara's blond hair and dark eyes like his and Claire's.

As if she could sense the change in him, a shy smile lit up Sara's face as she stepped closer. Before she reached him, a loud honking had everyone at the cookout turning toward the front of the house.

Josh could see a late-model sports car speeding up the long driveway that led to the main house, dust billowing behind it. Ryan's car.

A sliver of unease bracketed Josh's shoulders, but he ignored it. He didn't know what scheme Sara's former partner was cooking up tonight, but it didn't matter. Josh knew what he had to do.

He took the two steps to bring him to Sara's side. The scent of cinnamon and honey tantalized him, making his pulse stutter an erratic beat.

He wrapped his fingers around hers. "Sara, I need to talk to you."

"Sara!" Ryan's voice called from the front of the house.

She glanced up at Josh then to where Ryan was leaping onto the back patio.

"I have the most amazing news."

"Ryan, we have guests."

Ryan looked around for the first time, as if realizing there were other people at the house. Josh could sympathize. Sometimes when he looked at Sara everything else faded to nothing—that was how bright she glowed.

"Howdy, folks," Ryan said, then turned his attention back to Sara. "It's good there's a crowd. We're going to want to celebrate tonight. I talked to Jonathan Tramner today." He paused dramatically then raised his fists into the air. "He wants you," Ryan shouted. "He wants you for the part of Amelia!"

"That's impossible," Sara murmured.

Josh immediately released her hand and took a step back, feeling as though he was actually in a movie. He could see the scene in slow motion, him shouting an exaggerated no as the crowd looked on.

But this was real life and he kept his mouth shut, waiting to see how Sara would respond.

Ryan spoke before she could answer. "He loved your take on the character and said the short bit of the reading you did was fantastic." He glanced at Josh then back at Sara. "What made up his mind was the look on your face when you took the call about Claire. He said he saw Amelia in your face, all the motherly concern and love. He actually said it gave him chills."

Josh had chills right now. The bad kind, like right before you got sick to your stomach.

"I don't know what to say." Sara's hand fluttered to her chest as if to settle her breathing.

Josh kept his own breathing steady and even. Blood pumped through his veins, and he could have shot himself to the moon on pure adrenaline, but from the outside he knew he looked completely calm. It was a trick he'd mastered through decades of practice; whether it was his father coming after him as a kid or later when he was perched on the back of a bull, Josh earned a reputation for being cool under pressure.

The pressure on his heart right now threatened to overtake him.

"Say you'll accept the part. This is the kind of role that comes along once in a career, Sara. An award-winning kind of role." Ryan turned to the guests. "Give her some encouragement, everyone." Ryan's gaze met Josh's over her shoulder. "Our girl is going to be a star again."

Applause broke out around the small gathering, guests approaching Sara to offer their congratulations and words of encouragement. She might not get approval in L.A., but these people—strangers practically—were rooting for her. Josh guessed the rest of America would feel the same way. The country was built on comeback stories, and Sara would make a great one. She had talent but was smarter now. She wouldn't let anyone take advantage of her. She'd make career choices that would take her to the top.

Josh could see her future like a map and grew cold with the knowledge that it most likely didn't leave room for him.

He watched as April approached, taking Sara by the arms. "What are you going to do?" she asked softly.

"She's going to take the part," Ryan answered quickly. "She's wanted this for years. She deserves it."

"Let Sara decide," April told him sharply. "Think about it if you need to," she said to Sara in a gentler tone. "You don't have to give an answer right now."

Ryan tapped April on the shoulder. "Actually, she does. She reports to set next week."

"Next week?" Sara's gaze swung between April and Ryan. Josh felt himself sinking further into the background. Felt the walls he'd constructed for his own protection rebuilding, cutting off his heart. "Why so soon?" she asked. "I'm not ready to—"

Josh wanted to stop it, to swing her around and tell her everything he felt, all the plans he had for them. He wanted to beg her not to leave him. He couldn't, so he said nothing, stayed still as a statue while he watched her drift further away. The woman he hadn't believed would fit into his life only a month ago. Now he couldn't imagine living without her.

"Ready or not," Ryan answered. "They were already in preproduction when you met with Jonathan. He gave you a big break. The studio had a list of actresses they wanted. He fought for you, Sara. Do you know what that means?"

She nodded then turned to look at Josh as if to say, *Will you fight for me?*

Her eyes held a mix of hope, question and expectation. It was the last that did him in. After the accident, he'd felt broken and unfixable. He'd been given a second chance at life and with his daughter. But did he have enough to give to Sara, too?

He knew a life with her would mean revealing everything: his emotions, his heart. She'd want access to all the hidden crevices in his miserable soul. He could see it as he looked at her now, her gaze beginning to cloud as she read the doubt on his face. He was bound to disappoint her. He couldn't protect her, didn't have the guts to be the man she needed him to be. As much as he wished it was another way.

"Congratulations," he mumbled then forced a smile. "You deserve it."

Her breath hitched as she stared at him. All the people around them faded away as a single tear slid down her cheek. "So that's it?" she whispered.

He shrugged and ignored the pounding in his head. "Ryan's right. This is a once-in-a-lifetime chance. Take it." His throat felt like he'd swallowed a bucket of dust, but he didn't stop. "You don't belong here, Sara. I told you that from the start."

Sara clutched at her stomach, wondering if she might actually throw up. She didn't belong. Wasn't that the story of her life? Wasn't that what she thought she'd had here in Crimson with Josh? A place to call home for the first time.

Get a grip, her inner voice scolded and she bit down on her lip.

She turned to Ryan. "Make the call. I'll do it."

April reached for her hand, but she shrugged away, knowing if her friend touched her right now she might lose it completely. She'd gone soft this summer, let down her guard and her armor. That was the great thing about L.A., between the people and the traffic and the smog, she'd never questioned that every day would be a battle. She was used to it, ready to attack or go on the defensive no matter the situation.

Crimson Ranch and the mountains around it had lulled her into a false sense of security, made her believe she was safe in their shadow. She should have known better. She'd opened her heart and now she'd pay the price.

"You're crying." April handed Sara a napkin from a nearby table.

"Happy tears," she mumbled, praying she was a good enough actress to pull off this last scene. "Tears of joy for my dream come true." Her lips pulled into a wide smile. "I guess we have a real reason for a party now."

The guests cheered again, and Sara tried not to think about how much she'd miss meeting the vacationers who came to the ranch, hearing the stories of their lives. She'd already come to love the mornings when she walked across the property in the crisp mountain air to share a cup of coffee with April and any other early risers.

Yes, a part of her wanted her acting career back on track. She wanted to prove she was more than a washed-up child star. She wanted to lose herself in bringing a character to life again, stretch her range and know she could connect with the audience in that way.

Was it too much to want it all?

"How can you leave us?" Claire's angry voice broke her out of her musings. "You're dumping us, just like my mom did, for a better offer. Why does everyone leave me like I don't matter? I thought you were different."

"It's not like that," Sara whispered in response. Her heart broke all over again for the pain in the girl's eyes. Pain she'd caused.

Claire stood in front of her, chin trembling. Her arms were crossed in front of her chest.

Josh stepped forward, his entire focus on his daughter. "Sara was never going to stay," he told her, his voice a cool murmur.

I want to stay, she wanted to scream in response.

Ask me to stay.

Give me a reason to stay.

Claire turned to Sara. "You're a liar. You used us when you had nothing. You made me think you really cared."

Sara shook her head. "I do care, sweetie."

"You're as bad as my mother." Claire's big eyes narrowed. "As bad as your mother. I hate you."

Bile rose in Sara's throat at the comparison to Rose Wells. She'd been disappointed by her mother for so many years, she felt like it had broken something fundamental inside of her. She didn't trust her own judgment, her ability to form lasting relationships, her capacity for love.

This summer had gone a long way to fix what was wrong in her life. Or so she'd thought. Now she realized this was just one more illusion, like a movie set that could be stripped away in days—or in a moment—leaving a vast emptiness in its place.

But she didn't want that for Claire. She'd only wanted to spare the girl the pain Sara had felt for so many years.

She took a step forward but Josh blocked her way, putting himself between her and Claire, his back to Sara. Just like that, he cut her off from the two people she'd come to think of as hers. Guests drifted to the far side of the patio, making her feel even more alone.

"*We're* going to make this place work, Claire. You and me." Sara watched as he put his large hands on each of the girl's thin shoulders. "This is our home now. I'm not going to leave you. We're a team."

Sara had to physically restrain herself from rushing forward and wrapping her arms around them both. She ached to be part of their "team," as Josh called it. But here she was, once again on the sidelines.

Claire threw herself against her father's chest and sobbed out loud. The irony of the embrace wasn't lost on Sara. It had taken the two of them having a common enemy— her—for Claire to lean on Josh the way he'd wanted. She took no comfort in pushing the two of them together at last. Her pain was too raw for that. There was too much hurt between them all for her to believe this was the best ending to their story.

With his arm around Claire's shoulder, Josh led her from the porch.

Sara whispered his name and he turned. Fool that she was, she still held out a glimmer of hope that he'd call her to him and they'd work together to make this right.

Instead, his eyes held only derision as he looked at her. "You need to be out of here by tomorrow. I'll handle the bookings for the rest of the summer."

Pride made her chin notch up an inch. "It's my house."

A muscle in his jaw knotted. "I'll find a way to buy it from you. Before the end of the season."

No, she wanted to scream. That wasn't what she meant. "Josh, I don't..."

Her voice faded as she realized she was talking to his back. He and Claire disappeared into the house. Sara turned to April, miserable and needing her own comfort.

Even her best friend looked disappointed, as if Sara could have done better. How? How was she supposed to fight for something that wasn't hers to begin with?

Ever the peacekeeper, April turned to the guests, who'd gone silent. "It's still a beautiful night," April said, making her tone encouraging. "And we're happy each of you is here. I've got dinner ready in the kitchen." She smiled, and only Sara could see it didn't reach her eyes. "Who wants to load up a plate?"

The guests smiled and clapped and Sara felt a palpable easing of the tension. If April happened to be an X-Men type mutant under her braids and patchouli-scented sundresses, Sara would guess her superpower was making people feel better. She'd blessed Sara with her gift too many times to count, but never had she needed it more than now.

So when her friend turned and enveloped Sara in a hug, Sara sagged against her, wanting reassurance that she'd tried her best.

"What else could I do?" Sara asked, swallowing against the catch in her voice.

April pulled back and cupped Sara's face gently between her palms. Sara held her breath, waiting for the words of encouragement, the slant on the situation that would make Sara feel like a happy ending was still within reach.

"Make it right," April said simply, then turned and walked into the house to help the guests.

Sara whirled on Ryan. "What does she mean, make it right? I'm not the one who said I don't belong. I'm trying to make it right. I'm trying to resurrect my career, to pay her back the money you lost. I want the ranch to succeed. I want Claire to be okay. I want it all and I don't know how to get any of it. And she tells me to make it right?" She threw her hands in the air. "How do I do that, Ryan?"

He gave her a hug. "You start with what you should have done years ago. What I should have helped you accomplish. You take care of yourself."

The next morning, Sara folded her clothes and returned them to the suitcase she'd stowed in the back of the closet in her cabin.

She didn't go to the main house for breakfast, too emotionally drained to make small talk with the guests and too much of a coward to face April in the daylight.

As much of a nurturer as her friend was, April had made no secret last night that she thought Sara was making the wrong decision. Even if she hadn't said it out loud.

To Sara's surprise, April had told her she was going to stay on the ranch for the rest of the season. Apparently, Sara wasn't the only one who had experienced the healing power of the high mountain air. Sara had suggested that April contact Olivia Wilder to see about teaching yoga classes at the community center when it was complete.

Community.

It was a word that had held little meaning to Sara before this summer. With good reason, she realized now, since she clearly wasn't meant to be a part of this one.

Ryan was picking her up this morning to drive her to the airport, where she'd board a plane for the movie set. She was arriving a few days before shooting started, but an apartment had been rented for her and she wanted a chance to settle in before the rest of the cast and crew arrived. She also needed to get away from Colorado, from Josh and the dreams she'd been foolish enough to believe could come true for the two of them.

When a knock sounded on the door to the cabin, she called, "Come in," expecting to see Ryan. He was bringing by the contract and official paperwork for her to sign before they left.

Instead, her mother's voice rang out from the front room. "Serena, where are you? We need to talk."

Sara closed her eyes and took a steadying breath. The last person she wanted to speak to right now was her mother. But she walked from the bedroom into the main room of the cabin.

"Word travels fast," she said to Rose, who rushed forward to give her a hug.

"I'm thrilled for you, darling." Her mother smoothed back her hair with a frown and slight tsk of dissatisfaction. "We're not going to let this opportunity go to waste."

"*We're* not going to do anything," Sara replied, stepping out of her mother's embrace. "This has nothing to do with you."

"It has everything to do with me." Although Rose's voice was soft, Sara heard an edge of steel underneath. Her stomach did a slow roll, the same visceral reaction she'd had to her mother's unspoken demands since she was a girl.

"I'm your biggest fan," Rose continued. "Your first manager, you'll remember." She combed her fingers through her bangs. "It's time for me to get involved in your life again."

Sara's head snapped back as if she'd been slapped. "Not going to happen in a million years."

"Oh, yes. I think I may come to stay with you on set, for moral support and to make sure no one takes advantage of you. You're in a precarious place emotionally, since this is a chance you never thought you'd get." Her mother leaned forward. "Truth be told, you look quite ragged. Perhaps we could get you in for a bit of Botox before filming begins?"

Sara threw her arms into the air. "Mom, what are you talking about? I'm not getting Botox. You're not coming to the set."

"I have nothing else to occupy myself right now," her mother said with a sigh. "I'd planned to help Richard with plans for the condo development. I've always had an eye for interior design." She shrugged. "But since you won't sell the house yet, his deal has stalled. That leaves me free to focus my attention on you, my darling daughter." She tapped her finger on her upper lip. "And maybe Josh's daughter. I really do see potential in her. She obviously needs some maternal guidance."

"Leave Claire alone," Sara said on an angry hiss of breath. Temper flared to life inside her. "And get out of my life while you're at it."

"Give me a reason to," Rose shot back, the smile never leaving her face.

"Really, Mom? You're going to try to blackmail me now. That's a new low. It doesn't matter. I'm not afraid of you anymore and I don't need your approval. I haven't needed you for a long time."

Rose had the gall to look offended. "You'll always need me. I gave you the career you had."

"I worked for my career," Sara told her. "I had the talent you never did, and I worked for all the success I had. Unfortunately, I was naive enough to listen to you back then, to think you had my best interests at heart. Trust me, I won't make that mistake again."

She brushed past her mother and opened the front door. "I'm not going to sell the house, and there isn't a damn thing you can do about it. Now get out. For good, Mother. I don't want to see you here again."

"Don't do this, Sara," Rose said. Her voice turned to a pitiful whine. "I love Richard, but things are rocky between us since the land deal isn't working. I need you to help me."

Sara squeezed her eyes shut. This was the first time since she'd been a girl that her mother had called her by her given name. But even that small concession was too little, too late. "Get out," she repeated, sweeping her hand toward the porch.

With a dramatic sob, Rose rushed forward. "You'll change your mind," her mother called over her shoulder. "You can't do it on your own. You're not strong enough. You never were."

Sara sank onto the edge of the sofa, not bothering to shut the door behind her mother.

Those last angry words echoed through her as her head dropped to her knees, tears spilling down her face, soaking her bare legs. All the emotions, the hurt and betrayal, the disappointment over what would never be poured out of her.

After minutes, she gulped in an unsteady breath and raised her face, wiping her hands to clear the wetness.

"She's wrong," a voice said softly from the porch. Claire stood in the doorway, clenching her fingers at her sides. "You're strong enough. I believe in you, Sara."

Tears came again as Sara propelled herself off the couch, wrapping her arms around the girl. "I'm so sorry, sweetie. I never wanted to hurt you in all of this. I do care about you, Claire. I promise. Just because—"

"I know," Claire interrupted. "I was mad last night. I'm pretty sure the therapist my mom made me see would tell you I have some wicked abandonment issues." She laughed softly.

"Join the club." Sara pulled back. "We should introduce my mother to yours. They could start a mutual narcissistic personality club."

"If it keeps them busy..." Claire started.

"And off our backs," Sara finished.

They both laughed and Sara hugged her again. "You can call me on set. And text. And tweet. And Facebook. And whatever other ways to communicate they invent in the next five minutes. I'm sorry this summer didn't work out the way any of us planned, but I'm still your friend."

Claire nodded and blinked several times. "My dad isn't great at relationships. He won't let himself be vulnerable," she said, sounding far more mature than her thirteen years.

"Your therapist talking?"

"My mom. She talked a lot about him, mostly complaining. I think that's part of why I'm so hard on him. Years of conditioning, you know?"

Sara knew all about years of conditioning. That might explain why she was so hard on herself.

"He's a good man, Claire." The words ripped open a fresh flash of pain across Sara's heart. It made her ache to think of Josh, which was hard not to do on the ranch, when every smell and sound was bound together by her time with him. "He loves you."

"He loves you, too," Claire said firmly. "I know he does. He's just too much of a… man…to admit it."

"Common problem," Sara answered. "There's practically a whole subgenre of movies based on unhappy endings—*Gone with the Wind, Shakespeare in Love, Casablanca.*" She waved her hand, trying to be flip, then realized her fingers were trembling. She tucked her arm behind her back. "Our lives are too different to make it work."

"What about *Notting Hill?*" Claire's chin

jutted forward at a stubborn angle. "Julia Roberts and Hugh Grant made it work."

Sara couldn't help but smile. "I like the way your mind works, but this isn't the movies." She watched Claire push the toe of one shoe into the floor. "I promise you'll be okay. Your dad will make sure of it."

"I wish you didn't have to go," Claire said, hugging her again.

Sara willed herself to remain strong when all she wanted to do was melt into a weepy puddle once again. "Maybe you can come to the movie premiere." She paused, then added, "If your dad agrees."

Claire smiled through a hiccup. "If I'm on my best behavior, maybe he will." Then she giggled. "Do you think you could introduce me to Justin Timberlake?"

Sara laughed in response. "If I ever meet him, you bet."

Chapter Fifteen

"Can I go look at clothes?" Claire bounced on the tips of her toes as she smiled and nodded at Josh.

"At Feathers and Threads?" He arched a brow at her. "I thought you'd rather be seen in a potato sack."

"Don't be dramatic," his daughter answered, but her smile remained. "Sara told me they're carrying a couple of new lines." She bit her lip and glanced away.

Something that felt a lot like regret scraped across his insides at the mention of Sara's name. "I know you still talk to her and text. I monitor your phone even if I don't read them all, remember?"

"So annoying," Claire mumbled. "Can I go?"

"Sure." Josh glanced at his watch. "I need to load the rest of the wood into the truck, then I'll be down to pick you up."

"Thanks, Dad."

He watched his daughter cross the street toward the boutique on the corner. He felt a lightness fill his chest at the change in his relationship with Claire. It was followed quickly by the weight of knowing that Sara had a lot to do with the progress.

It had been three weeks since she'd left Crimson. Almost a month filled with emptiness and a constant longing to be with her again. He hoped it would fade soon, or he thought he might go mad from the pain of it. Pain he knew he'd caused himself.

He knew what she'd wanted that night on the patio. Her eyes had held a hope that he'd offer more. He'd wanted to, planned on it until Ryan had come in with his big announcement. How could Josh compete with the bright lights of Hollywood?

He cursed under his breath. When had he ever backed away from a fight? He knew it was a mistake, but in that moment he couldn't stop himself from making it.

He wouldn't ask her to give up another chance at her career. Yet he hadn't been able to offer her the relationship she deserved, because he was too afraid that when she was away filming, he couldn't protect her. It hadn't worked with his sister or with his relationship with Claire's mother. Here in Colorado, on the ranch, he could make sure everything was okay for the people he loved. He was in charge of his life and emotions. Things were simple, just the way he liked them. He was too afraid of losing her when she left him. Too scared she'd eventually choose her career over him.

As much as he knew now that he loved Sara with his whole heart, he'd tried to convince himself it was for the best. The whole reason he'd returned to Crimson was to protect Claire, to give her the normal life he'd always craved. Not to let the outside world seep in and destroy them.

It was irrational, he knew. Sara had been a positive influence on his daughter from the start. But he held on to his fear like an anchor and only now worried it might take him down, as well.

"You got a lot of posts there. Not sure you'll need that many."

Josh looked up into the face of Richard Hamish, partially shaded by the large Stetson on his head. "You have no idea what I need, Rich." Josh took a pair of work gloves from his back pocket and slipped them on. "Go play intimidating cowboy with someone else. It's wasted on me." He hefted several boards into the truck bed. "If you haven't heard, Crimson Ranch is having a great first season. I'm going to secure that loan and buy the house come fall."

"Not if she sells it to me first."

The older man sounded as if it were a done deal, confidence dripping from every syllable.

"You're bluffing." Josh kept working on loading fence posts into the truck, needing to keep his hands occupied so he wasn't tempted to wrap them around Richard's craggy neck. "Sara isn't going to sell you the house. Not now."

"Rose flew down there and is working on her as we speak."

Josh stilled. "On set with Sara?" He knew how much being near her mother upset Sara.

She didn't need that kind of distraction when she was filming a movie.

"I sure as hell don't want Rose around me until this deal goes through." Richard spit a wad of tobacco into the street. "Dang woman talks my ear off. She meddles into every detail of a man's life. It's about time she uses her energy on someone other than me. She can wear that girl down. I'd bet my belt buckle on it."

"You think Rose will convince Sara to sell?"

"Her mom will head back here once Sara agrees."

"She won't do it." Josh wanted to be sure, but how could he? He'd given Sara no reason to believe in him. Why should she stick to their bargain at this point? If she wanted to get on with her life, the easiest path would be to sign the house over to her mother.

"If she wants to keep that fancy new movie role, she will."

"Sara earned that part. Even if her mother is an annoyance, she's not going to cost her the job."

Richard's smile was too confident. "Sara's had a bumpy few years. There's a lot of pressure trying to restart a life. You should understand that better than most. Who knows if she can handle it? She may crack, go back to using drugs—"

"She didn't use drugs and you know it."

"Doesn't matter what I know. The important thing is what the American people believe. One story in the tabloids and that production company will drop her in an instant."

Josh took a step forward, stripping off his gloves and grabbing Richard by the collar of his custom Western shirt. "You wouldn't…" His voice was a low growl.

"Who's going to stop me?" He pulled away from Josh's grasp. "Son, you've been outplayed."

Without thinking, Josh slammed his fist into the other man's jaw. Richard staggered back into the brick storefront. Several men rushed out of the hardware store to see what the commotion was.

"This isn't a game, you old coot." Josh shook out his hand, glancing at his knuckles where a few trickles of blood pooled.

"It's her life. And to answer the question of who's going to stop you?" He came close to Richard, who cradled his face in his palm. "That would be me."

* * *

Sara held her fingers to her ears, but even that couldn't drown out her mother's incessant rambling.

"I talked to craft services about your food allergies and exactly what they need to stock for you."

Sara's head shot up. "I don't have food allergies."

"Sensitivities, then."

"I'm only sensitive to your voice." She got up from the couch in her on-set trailer. "When is this going to end, Mother?"

When Rose had first arrived three days ago, Sara had refused to let her on set. But Rose took matters into her own hands, meeting with the director and one of the executive producers to spin a tale of Sara's fragile emotional state and how Rose wanted to make sure she didn't cost them money on the movie.

What Rose was going to cost Sara was her sanity.

Thanks to Sara's less-than-stellar reputation, the men had believed it. Rose had become a constant presence during filming. It was hard for Sara to stay connected with the character of a hardworking mom when all she wanted was for her own mother to leave her the hell alone.

"You know what it takes," Rose said simply, turning to the small bank of cabinets she was rearranging.

Rose had even gotten Jonathan Tramner, the director, to suggest to Sara that her mother stay with her in the studio apartment at the end of filming each day. Sara got no break, which was making her crazy.

"Why is Richard Hamish so important that you'll do anything to make me sell Gran's house to him?"

"I love him."

"It would be a revelation if you loved your own daughter half as much."

Rose didn't turn around, but her shoulders stiffened. "I do love you, Serena. I devoted my life to making your career a success. You owe me for that."

"I paid the bills for a decade." Resentment rose hot and strong in Sara. "I more than paid my debt to you." When her mother didn't turn around, Sara's gaze fell to the line of glass bottles on the small cabinet.

"Why is all that liquor in here?"

"One of the men helped me unload it." Her mother's voice was emotionless. "I explained to them that you might need a little something to calm your nerves."

"My nerves wouldn't be so shot if you'd leave. And you know I do yoga for…" Her voice trailed off as realization dawned. "You're going to make it seem like I'm a drunk?" She stood, pacing the small room. "Do you have needles stashed somewhere, too?"

"Sell the house." Rose spun around, her finger pointed in accusation. "Why are *you* so devoted to a man who doesn't want you? You're going to save his ranch and let my dream for a happy life be thrown in the trash. You shouldn't be protecting him. He doesn't care about you, Serena. You're not important to him. When are you going to stop being a doormat for people who are only using you?"

The air whooshed out of the room, and Sara thought her knees might buckle. Her mother was right. She was a doormat. No matter how tough she talked, how insolent her attitude, she let people take advantage of her. Her mother was first in that line.

Maybe that was what Josh had been doing, wooing her in Colorado to ensure her loyalty. It didn't matter anymore. Her time with him had given her the confidence to believe in herself again. Even if he didn't believe in the two of them, he'd given her a gift she could never repay.

"Good point, Mom." She pushed open the door to the trailer. "First I'm going to stop being a doormat for you."

"I didn't mean…"

"I don't care." She lifted her hands. "I don't care if you ruin my career. Again. If they fire me, I'll find another job, another path. Even if it isn't in Hollywood. I love acting, not being a celebrity." She thought about Olivia's offer to help with the community theater in Crimson. "I can make my life a success. I deserve happiness, and I'm not going to let you rob me of it for one second longer."

"You don't know what you're saying."

"She does."

Sara whirled as Josh filled the tiny doorway of the trailer. His gaze was fixed on Rose. "She should have said it a long time ago. I should have said it for her. To her." He turned to Sara. "You deserve happiness."

Rose stalked forward. "You only want the house. You don't care about her."

His eyes never left Sara's. "Sell the house."

She shook her head.

"I mean it," he said, and took her arms between his hands. Close enough that she could see the tiny flecks of gold in his dark eyes. Close enough that the smell of him wound through her senses like a drug. "Sell the house if it will make you happy."

"It's your future," she said softly.

"I'll make a different future," he answered. "With you, if you'll have me. No piece of property, no business is worth anything without you in my life to share it. I love you, Sara. I think I have since the moment you jumped on the counter and spun my world out of control."

She drew a shaky breath, unable to believe what she was hearing. "But you like control."

"I thought I needed it," he said, pushing a stray hair behind her ear. His touch made a shiver run through her. "I'm sorry for hurting you and letting you walk away." He dipped his head so he was looking directly into her eyes. "I was wrong about a lot of things. But one thing I'm definitely right about is that nothing is worth losing you."

She choked back a sob and tried to look away. He held her head steady. "Claire loves you. I love you. We both need you in our lives so damn much. Please give us another chance, Sara. Name the terms. Anything you want."

She shook her head. "I can't cook," she mumbled.

One side of his mouth kicked up. "We'll order takeout."

"I'm opinionated."

"I want to hear every thought in that beautiful mind."

Her eyes searched his. She saw the truth of his words, of his love for her. Still, she was so scared to risk having her heart and dreams crushed once more. She didn't know if she could survive again.

"I want to act," she told him, wondering if it would be the nail in the coffin.

He leaned forward and ran his lips against hers. "I'll be at every premiere and production. I'll help you learn lines. I'll come to you wherever you are." His soft breath fell against her mouth. "Because I'm nothing without you, Sara. Wherever you are is where I want to be. Forever."

Her arms wrapped around his waist, and he pulled her to him, deepening the kiss until she was lost in sensation. "I love you, Josh," she said after a moment. "Forever."

"Well, that was a scene worthy of a Lifetime movie if I've ever seen one."

Her mother's sarcastic voice cut into Sara's bliss like a blade.

Josh held her to him, dropping a kiss on her forehead. "It's real, Rose. You wouldn't recognize real love, and I'm sorry for that." He met her mother's angry gaze. "I love your daughter and I won't let you hurt her anymore."

"Easy to say when you get what you want in the end."

"What I want is Sara's happiness."

"What you get is the house that should have been mine."

He looked down into Sara's eyes. "I meant what I said. Sell the house if it will make things easier for you. I'll find another property. We'll rebuild. As long as you're with me, I can make it right."

She shook her head. "It's right just the way it is."

Turning to Rose, she said, "I'm not selling, Mom. You can't blackmail me into it. You can't threaten. I'm not giving you power over me again."

"We'll see what happens when Richard takes control of this," her mother spit out, pulling out her cell phone and punching in numbers. "You always were ungrateful."

"I don't think you'll get a hold of him right now," Josh said casually. "He flew down to Houston this morning to see his wife."

Rose's hand stilled in midair. "Wife?"

"You didn't know? Yes, his wife of twenty-five years lives in Texas. Didn't you think it was odd how he never took you with him when he flew down there?"

"Those were business trips," Rose said woodenly.

"You were the one being used, Mom," Sara said. "I'm sorry."

Rose shook her head. "I don't need your pity."

"I don't pity you," Sara explained. "I'm sorry you think so little of yourself that you let a man treat you like that."

"That house should still be mine."

"It's not and it's never going to be. Move on, Mother."

Rose looked around the trailer as if not really seeing anything. "I need help. I need the house."

"Yes," Sara agreed. "You need to learn to stand on your own two feet. Trust me—that's the best help I can give you."

Rose's spine stiffened. "Once I walk out

that door, you're dead to me, Serena. Be careful what you choose right now."

Sara didn't hesitate in her response. "I choose love," she whispered, and pressed her cheek against Josh's warm chest.

With a muttered curse, Rose fled from the trailer, slamming the door behind her.

Josh tipped her head up. "Forever?"

She nodded. "I choose you, Josh Travers. Forever."

* * * * *

HOME *on the* RANCH

YES! Please send me the **Home on the Ranch Collection** in Larger Print. This collection begins with 3 FREE books and 2 FREE gifts in the first shipment. Along with my 3 free books, I'll also get the next 4 books from the Home on the Ranch Collection, in LARGER PRINT, which I may either return and owe nothing, or keep for the low price of $5.24 U.S./ $5.89 CDN each plus $2.99 for shipping and handling per shipment*. If I decide to continue, about once a month for 8 months I will get 6 or 7 more books, but will only need to pay for 4. That means 2 or 3 books in every shipment will be FREE! If I decide to keep the entire collection, I'll have paid for only 32 books because 19 books are FREE! I understand that accepting the 3 free books and gifts places me under no obligation to buy anything. I can always return a shipment and cancel at any time. My free books and gifts are mine to keep no matter what I decide.

268 HCN 3760 468 HCN 3760

Name	(PLEASE PRINT)	
Address		Apt. #
City	State/Prov.	Zip/Postal Code

Signature (if under 18, a parent or guardian must sign)

Mail to the **Reader Service**:

IN U.S.A.: P.O. Box 1341, Buffalo, New York 14240-8531
IN CANADA: P.O. Box 603, Fort Erie, Ontario L2A 5X3

* Terms and prices subject to change without notice. Prices do not include applicable taxes. Sales tax applicable in NY. Canadian residents will be charged applicable taxes. This offer is limited to one order per household. All orders subject to approval. Credit or debit balances in a customer's account(s) may be offset by any other outstanding balance owed by or to the customer. Please allow 3 to 4 weeks for delivery. Offer available while quantities last. Offer not available to Quebec residents.

Your Privacy—The Reader Service is committed to protecting your privacy. Our Privacy Policy is available online at www.ReaderService.com or upon request from the Reader Service.

We make a portion of our mailing list available to reputable third parties that offer products we believe may interest you. If you prefer that we not exchange your name with third parties, or if you wish to clarify or modify your communication preferences, please visit us at www.ReaderService.com/consumerschoice or write to us at Reader Service Preference Service, P.O. Box 9062, Buffalo, NY. 14240-9062. Include your complete name and address.

HRCBPA18R

Get 4 FREE REWARDS!

We'll send you 2 FREE Books
<u>plus</u> 2 FREE Mystery Gifts.

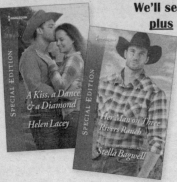

Harlequin® Special Edition books feature heroines finding the balance between their work life and personal life on the way to finding true love.

FREE
Value Over
$20

Get 4 FREE REWARDS!

We'll send you 2 FREE Books plus 2 FREE Mystery Gifts.

Harlequin® Heartwarming™ Larger-Print books feature traditional values of home, family, community and most of all—love.

FREE
Value Over
$20

YES! Please send me 2 FREE Harlequin® Heartwarming™ Larger-Print novels and my 2 FREE mystery gifts (gifts worth about $10 retail). After receiving them, if I don't wish to receive any more books, I can return the shipping statement marked "cancel." If I don't cancel, I will receive 4 brand-new larger-print novels every month and be billed just $5.49 per book in the U.S. or $6.24 per book in Canada. That's a savings of at least 19% off the cover price. It's quite a bargain! Shipping and handling is just 50¢ per book in the U.S. and 75¢ per book in Canada*. I understand that accepting the 2 free books and gifts places me under no obligation to buy anything. I can always return a shipment and cancel at any time. The free books and gifts are mine to keep no matter what I decide.

161/361 IDN GMY3

Name (please print)

Address   Apt. #

City   State/Province   Zip/Postal Code

> Mail to the **Reader Service:**
> **IN U.S.A.:** P.O. Box 1341, Buffalo, NY 14240-8531
> **IN CANADA:** P.O. Box 603, Fort Erie, Ontario L2A 5X3

Want to try two free books from another series? Call 1-800-873-8635 or visit www.ReaderService.com.

---

*Terms and prices subject to change without notice. Prices do not include applicable taxes. Sales tax applicable in N.Y. Canadian residents will be charged applicable taxes. Offer not valid in Quebec. This offer is limited to one order per household. Books received may not be as shown. Not valid for current subscribers to Harlequin Heartwarming Larger-Print books. All orders subject to approval. Credit or debit balances in a customer's account(s) may be offset by any other outstanding balance owed by or to the customer. Please allow 4 to 6 weeks for delivery. Offer available while quantities last.

Your Privacy—The Reader Service is committed to protecting your privacy. Our Privacy Policy is available online at www.ReaderService.com or upon request from the Reader Service. We make a portion of our mailing list available to reputable third parties that offer products we believe may interest you. If you prefer that we not exchange your name with third parties, or if you wish to clarify or modify your communication preferences, please visit us at www.ReaderService.com/consumerschoice or write to us at Reader Service Preference Service, P.O. Box 9062, Buffalo, NY 14240-9062. Include your complete name and address.

HW18

READERSERVICE.COM

Manage your account online!

- Review your order history
- Manage your payments
- Update your address

We've designed the
Reader Service website
just for you.

Enjoy all the features!

- Discover new series available to you, and read excerpts from any series.
- Respond to mailings and special monthly offers.
- Browse the Bonus Bucks catalog and online-only exculsives.
- Share your feedback.

Visit us at:

ReaderService.com

RS16R